CATCHING BETSY

Mail-Order Grooms, Book 2

AMELIA SMARTS

Published by Amelia Smarts
ameliasmarts.com

Smarts, Amelia
Catching Betsy

Cover Design by germancreative
Images by The Killion Group, Inc.

ISBN: 9781548543730

Chapter One

Nevada, 1898

Betsy Blake walked into the kitchen and stopped abruptly as her mouth dropped open in horror. The Harringtons' four-year-old daughter was stuffing a fistful of blueberry pie into her mouth, smearing crumbs and fruit around her face. The child had grabbed a handful right from the center of the pie, effectively ruining it.

Betsy groaned. "Oh, Mini! Your ma said you weren't to eat that."

Virginia Harrington, first nicknamed Ginny, which then led to the pet name "Mini" on account of her tiny stature, grinned without remorse. "It's yummy, Miss Betsy. Want some?" She held out her chubby fist filled with crust and fruit. Blueberry oozed through her fingers, dropping dollops of goo onto the floor.

"Sakes alive." Betsy held her palms to her face. She couldn't believe she'd let this happen. As often as she'd watched the Harrington children, she should have

1

known to keep better watch over the younger child, who was a peck of trouble on the best of days. But Caleb, her older brother, had needed help with his arithmetic and she'd lost track of the little troublemaker. "Your parents are going to flay me, Mini. Thanks a lot."

As if summoned to the task, Adam's and Susannah's buggy squeaked to a halt outside. They were already home from their supper in town, not even giving Betsy enough time to clean up the mess. The little girl quickly made herself scarce, dashing out of the kitchen as soon as she heard the horse's nicker and leaving Betsy to face them alone.

Betsy drew a deep breath and tried to settle her nerves. Susannah had always been like an older sister to her, and she likely wouldn't stay cross for long. But Adam was known for intolerance when it came to mistakes. She knew this because her pa was the foreman of the Harringtons' ranch and Adam was his boss. Adam was strict when it came to his ranch hands and his business, and he was quick to let a man go if he wasn't up to snuff.

Betsy enjoyed watching the children to earn spending money and didn't want her job to end, but fear of getting fired wasn't her main source of dismay. She wanted Adam to like her because she'd always respected him. Some five years back, he'd traveled all the way from Amarillo to Virginia City to marry Susannah, and his forbidding, no-nonsense attitude had made an immediate impression on everyone in town, including Betsy. People joked behind his back that he was a mail-order groom because he'd responded to an advertisement Susannah had placed in the paper asking for a rancher husband, but they didn't repeat the same jokes to his face.

Now that Betsy was a grown woman of eighteen and thinking about marriage herself, she thought Susannah had been smart to find a husband in that manner. A couple local suitors had asked Betsy's pa for permission to court her, but she wasn't interested in them. One in particular, a ranch hand named Johnny, still insisted on coming around even after she gave him the mitten. At best he would annoy her. At worst he would disgust her.

Johnny's topics of conversation never centered around anything she was interested in, such as music or art. He spoke loudly over her, bragging that he was the most skilled out of all Adam's cowhands. He also made sure to point out that he deserved a much more lucrative occupation, since he'd received high marks in school and would have done well in college if he'd been able to afford it. It was only his lack of funds that prevented him from getting anywhere further in life. His face would twist into a grimace, expressing great bitterness at the world for his lot.

After every one of these conversations, Betsy was convinced more than ever that she wanted to marry a gentleman, not a cowboy, and gentlemen were hard to find in Virginia City. Writing an advertisement specifying exactly the kind of man she wanted—someone from the east with good table manners who didn't smell like cows or sweat—held great appeal.

"Hello, Betsy!" The back door rattled open and in walked Susannah, followed by Adam, who closed the door behind them. Susannah appeared flushed and happy, with a big smile on her face, but her smile quickly faded when she spotted what was left of her pie on the table.

"I'm sorry, Mrs. Harrington!" Betsy cried. "I wasn't watching Mini as I should have been because I was helping Caleb with his homework in the other room."

Susannah sank onto the stool next to the table, appearing suddenly weary, though still as beautiful as ever. Her blonde hair, which Betsy had always admired, cascaded in perfect waves around her shoulders. Betsy thought her own hair was decidedly average in comparison—straight, dark, and long, worn in a single braid down her back.

Adam frowned at the pie before looking at Susannah and saying, "I thought you told Mini not to touch it because it was for the potluck tomorrow."

"I did," Susannah replied, scowling at him, "and she didn't care. You're too lenient with her. She knows she can get away with anything."

Adam didn't deny it. He leaned back against the counter and scraped his fingers through his dark hair.

Betsy felt near tears. She hated seeing Susannah so upset. "Please forgive me, Mrs. Harrington. I promise I'll do a better job of watching her next time."

"It's not your fault," Adam said gruffly. "Mini knows right from wrong."

"Yes, she does," Susannah agreed, "and we're the ones raising a little hellion." She stood and walked to the door. "Mini! Come here, please."

She returned to sitting on the stool next to the ruined pie while they waited for the youngest Harrington.

Her tiny footsteps could be heard getting closer. Before the girl walked in, Susannah said to Adam, "I know she's cute and can be as sweet as… well, pie. But she's so naughty. You have to be firm with her this time."

Adam nodded. "I will be, darlin'."

A shiver went through Betsy, and she looked longingly at the back door, trying to determine if there was a graceful way to exit. She didn't relish the thought of being around while Adam was firm with anyone, let alone his daughter who she was fond of, even if she was bad sometimes.

Before Betsy could make her escape, the little girl walked in and glanced around the room with wide, brown eyes. She was an adorable child and a near equal blend of both her parents. She had Susannah's fair skin and button nose and her father's brown eyes and dark hair. Ringlets curled around her heart-shaped face. Both of her chubby cheeks and her lips were stained purple, as was the hand that had grabbed the pie.

Susannah pointed at the ruined dessert. "Mini, did you eat the pie I told you was for the potluck tomorrow?" It was a question everyone knew the answer to, of course, especially considering the proof smeared all over the child's face.

Mini looked at the pie, then back at her ma and shook her head. "No, Mama, I didn't eat it. I saw a 'coon tryin' to get in through the door while you were fixin' to leave. I shooed it away, but I reckon it scooted in later and ate your pie."

Adam coughed and turned his head away quickly, but not before Betsy saw the smile he tried to hide. She relaxed a little, guessing that Adam likely wouldn't be too harsh with Mini if he was feeling amused instead of angry.

Susannah, however, wasn't impressed in the least. "Adam!" she exclaimed. "Did you hear that balderdash coming from your child?"

Adam cleared his throat and adopted a sober expression, with difficulty it seemed. "I did. Come here, Mini."

Mini skipped to him without reservation, not seeming the least bit concerned about being in trouble with her pa. Adam scooped her up and set her on the counter. He picked up a strip of cloth and dipped it into the water basin. After wringing it out, he applied it to Mini's cheeks and mouth. "You know what I'm doing right now?"

"Yeah," she said, giggling. "You're washing my face, Pa."

"That's right. I'm washing the blueberry pie off your face." His mouth formed into a firm line, but his eyes twinkled hopelessly.

Mini stopped giggling, suddenly seeming to understand that she wasn't going to get away with her stunt. Her gaze darted between her parents as Adam cleaned her up.

Setting the cloth aside, Adam repeated Susannah's question in a stern voice. "Did you eat the pie after your ma told you not to, Virginia?"

Mini's eyes flooded with tears. "Yes, Pa."

Adam raised a brow. "So not only did you eat your ma's pie, you also lied about it when you tried to blame a raccoon, didn't you?"

Her lower lip quivered before she whispered, "Yes." She looked down at her hands, which were clutching and twisting her skirt.

"You know better than to lie to your ma, and you know better than to disobey. Now no one at the potluck will be able to eat pie because Mama doesn't have time to bake another one. What if Mrs. Pierce wanted some or your friend Clara? Now they won't get any."

"They won't?" she asked in a small voice, sounding devastated.

Betsy's heart went out to the girl, who didn't seem to understand until that moment that her actions could have any negative effect on others. She could be naughty, but she wasn't mean-spirited.

Adam must have thought the same. His voice gentled. "No they won't, honey. That's why your ma told you to leave it alone 'til tomorrow, so that other people can enjoy it."

She let out an anguished sob and leaned forward to bury her face against his chest. "I want Mrs. Pierce and Clara to have pie too. Please can you give them some?"

"They're going to have to wait until the next potluck, when Mama will bake another. And you're not going to ruin that one, are you?"

"No!" she sobbed.

Adam wrapped his arms around her and pulled her off the counter. She clung to him and cried, her legs wrapped tightly around his waist and her arms around his neck. He glanced at Susannah with something like a helpless expression. It was clear he was undone by his daughter's tears. He rubbed her back and held her until she calmed down, then set her on her feet in front of him. She stared up at him with red-rimmed eyes and a runny nose, hiccupping and twisting the hem of her dress in one hand.

She looked so tiny and vulnerable in the room full of adults, all of whom were focused on her and her wrongdoing. Adam regarded her mournfully for a moment. Finally, he sighed and said, "Go say you're sorry to your ma and then go straight to bed, Mini. I expect you to be obedient and honest from now on. Is that understood?"

She nodded and sniffled.

"Yes, Pa?" he prompted.

"Yes, Pa," she repeated.

"Go on then."

Mini trudged to her ma and apologized through hiccups, sounding very remorseful, which caused Susannah's gaze to soften. Neither of her parents could stay upset with her for long, it seemed. After Mini left the room to go to bed, Susannah rolled her eyes. "Well, you sure told her."

Adam chuckled and shook his head. "I'm sorry. I should have punished her with more than an early bedtime for that, but it was hard enough for me to scold her. Then when she starting crying and looking at me with those big, sad eyes…"

Susannah scoffed and addressed Betsy. "He wasn't always this lenient. He's gone soft."

Betsy grinned, enjoying the lighthearted direction the conversation had taken, and also greatly relieved that Adam had been so lenient with the little girl.

Adam grunted. "That's because you and Caleb plumb wore me out. Where is that boy, anyway? I don't reckon he's ever stayed away from the kitchen this long before."

"Oh, he'll be here shortly, I'm sure. You should pay Betsy so that she can get on home. Sorry for keeping you, honey."

"We appreciate you being here," Adam said, and retrieved his wallet. "As you can imagine, it does me and Susannah good to get away from the kids for a spell." He handed Betsy her pay as Caleb joined them in the kitchen. Now a strapping boy of ten years old, Betsy remembered him at Mini's age, which was when Adam had come to marry Susannah and be a father to the little boy.

Caleb looked at the pie, and his eyebrows shot up. "Mini's doing?"

When everyone nodded, he asked, "Don't suppose I could eat some?"

"Go right ahead," Susannah said, waving her hand at the mess. "Not taking that to the potluck."

Caleb grabbed a fork, sat down on a stool next to his ma, and dug in. "Delicious!" he reported. After swallowing his first large bite, he asked, "Pa, can I go fishing with William tomorrow?"

"Don't see why not," Adam said. "Did you finish your homework?"

He nodded. "Yup, all done."

Mini returned to the kitchen then, her eyes dried and cheerful demeanor returned. Adam frowned at her. "Didn't I say to go to bed?"

"I wanted to say goodnight to Miss Betsy," she explained, and wrapped her arms around Betsy's waist.

Betsy returned the hug. "Sweet dreams, Mini. I'll see you tomorrow at the potluck, all right?"

"All right." Mini released her hold on Betsy.

Caleb set down his fork. "Say Pa, can you help me find worms tomorrow before I go to the fishing hole?"

Before Adam could respond, Mini spun around and exclaimed, "I wanna go fishing too, Caleb!"

He glared at her. "No! You're not coming, Mini. You'll only get in the way."

For the second time that evening, Mini's eyes filled with tears. "Ma, make Caleb say I can go with him!"

Susannah let out an exasperated sigh. "Your pa will take you fishing another time. Go to bed, Mini. You're tired."

She dropped to the floor and wailed, "But I want to go fishing with Caleb!"

Adam groaned and strode forward to pick her up off the ground. She laid her head on his shoulder as he chided her. "You can't always get what you want, Mini, and that's no reason to pitch a fit."

She only cried in response.

"Such big feelings for such a little girl, huh?"

"Yes," she sobbed. "Caleb is mean and he never wants to play with me."

Adam frowned at Caleb. "I expect you to be a little gentler with your sister, son. She only wants to spend time with you because she looks up to you."

"I didn't mean to make her cry," he grumbled.

"I know, but there was a nicer way to tell her she couldn't come. Maybe you could have offered to stack blocks with her tomorrow for a few minutes instead."

A look of resignation crossed Caleb's face. "I could do that. I'm sorry, Mini."

"I-I forgive y-you," she said magnanimously through her tears, her head still resting on Adam's shoulder.

Adam's lips quirked up briefly and he winked at Caleb. "All right, that's settled and it's this one's bedtime," he announced, heading for the door. "Betsy, you have a good night now."

"Thank you, Mr. Harrington. You too."

Betsy turned to Susannah. "Sorry again about your pie, Mrs. Harrington. I'm glad Mr. Harrington wasn't too hard on Mini. I would've felt even more terrible."

Susannah smiled and shook her head. "He's a good father, even when he's hard on the children. Never loses his temper and is always fair."

"I hope to get married to a nice man soon," Betsy said. She picked up her duster from where it hung over a chair and shrugged her arms into it.

"I imagine a pretty girl like you is attracting suitors like bees to honey."

Betsy giggled. "There are a few men who are interested in seeing me, but the trouble is, I don't like any of them. They're immature and dirty and they smell like cowboys."

Susannah threw back her head and laughed. "Well, honey, that's probably 'cause they *are* cowboys. And cowboys can be washed, you know."

She shrugged. "I suppose, but I wish I could meet a gentleman, like someone from the east who dresses in fine clothes. Maybe a musician or a businessman." Betsy pulled the duster around her tightly. It was chilly outside, but she didn't have far to walk. Her parents' house was within sight of the Harringtons'.

"Now that sounds nice and all, but you have to make sure he can earn a living, not just strut around in fine clothes," Susannah admonished. "With cowboys, you know they can take care of a family because they work hard to earn their pennies."

"Yes, ma'am, that's what my parents say."

Betsy considered sharing with Susannah that she'd been thinking about putting a mail-order groom ad in the paper just like Susannah had done, but she decided against it. She didn't want Susannah to laugh or try to discourage her, so she said goodbye and headed home.

The wind howled around her, and Betsy shivered and quickened her steps toward the cabin. Because her head was bent down, it came as a surprise when Johnny Miller suddenly stepped out from behind a tree in front of her, preventing her journey to her cabin from continuing. "Hello, sweet thang," Johnny drawled. "Nice evening for a walk."

"Hello," she said politely, and tried to step around him, but he sidestepped and prevented her from moving forward. She sighed. "Please let me pass, Johnny. I'm cold and I want to go home."

"What's the big hurry? Seems you're always in a rush whenever I wanna talk to you."

A whiff of cow manure filled her nostrils. Likely it was stuck to his clothing. She wrinkled her nose in disgust as her annoyance bubbled to the surface. Why wouldn't he get the hint and leave her alone? Betsy had been taught to be polite and nice to everyone, but doing so with Johnny had only caused his attention to continue. Perhaps it was time to be a little more forceful.

"I always seem in a rush because I don't want to talk to you," she said firmly. "I've told you I'm not interested in courting you, but you don't seem to believe me."

It was likely the rudest thing Betsy had ever said in her life, but she didn't know how else to make her feelings clear. She watched as Johnny's fair cheeks flushed red, and she felt a tug at her conscience. She didn't want to hurt his feelings or humiliate him, and it was clear she had from the look on his face.

"You think you're something special, don't you? Think you're too good for me." He spat the words, his eyes flashing with hurt and something else—anger. Betsy felt alarmed by his expression.

She looked around, feeling alone suddenly, and cleared her throat. "I don't think I'm too good for you, I'm just looking for a different type of man," she explained in conciliatory tones. "I'm sure you'll find a real nice girl, Johnny."

Her explanation only seemed to make him angrier. He loomed over her, and Betsy noticed for the first time how tall he was. "You're going to regret being such an offish bitch to me," he snarled.

She swallowed, her throat dry, and took a step back. Her mind raced. She was closer to the Harringtons' cabin than to her own. Her instincts told her to run, but she hesitated, thinking perhaps that would be overreacting. Johnny was annoying, but surely he wouldn't actually hurt her.

She'd no sooner thought that when he reached out and clutched her arm with a hard grip. Her heartbeat quickened. His hold on her felt out of control, like he didn't understand his own strength. "Let me go, Johnny!"

He didn't. Instead, he shook her. "No one will treat you as good as I will, if you'll only let me prove it," he told her, a desperate look on his face. The irony of him saying that while hurting her escaped him.

Trying to wrench her arm free was of no use. She whimpered when he squeezed even tighter. A moment later she saw his eyes widen, and then he released her. She took that opportunity to run back toward the Harringtons' cabin. In doing so, she turned and collided with Adam, who had come up upon them unbeknownst to her. She rammed into him with such force that he had to reach out and steady her to keep her from bouncing off him and falling to the ground. She nearly cried with relief.

Adam kept a hand on her shoulder and spoke to Johnny. "What's going on here?"

The sound of Adam's voice made Betsy shiver. She couldn't remember ever hearing him sound so cold and threatening, and she was reminded in that moment why her pa always said he was a hard man.

"Nothing, sir," Johnny said, his cheeks still red. "I was just saying hello to Miss Blake."

"Yeah? You have an interesting way of doing that. Did he hurt you, Betsy?"

Betsy's entire body was trembling, and tears came to her eyes. She opened her mouth to speak but couldn't find the words. She didn't want to get Johnny into trouble. She just wanted him to leave her alone. Now that his boss was involved, one word from her could mean a loss of his job. When she looked at Adam, he was staring at her with concern.

He seemed to know all that was needed with his own observations. He gave Johnny a hard stare. "Get out of here, and don't come back unless you plan to go to the doctor directly after. Consider yourself fired."

His jaw dropped. "But, Mr. Harrington, I didn't mean…"

Adam removed his hand from Betsy's shoulder, stepped forward, and grabbed Johnny by his collar. "You'd better start making tracks before I make you buzzard bait. After what I saw, you grabbing Betsy's arm like that, you're lucky I don't report you to the marshal. I still might. *Leave!*"

When Adam released him, Johnny spat on the ground and turned to walk away, giving Betsy a wounded, angry look before he left.

Betsy stared after him. She still couldn't find her tongue, but Adam didn't expect her to speak. He only patted her shoulder and said, "Come on, I'll take you home and you can tell your pa what happened." He led the way toward Betsy's house, a grim expression on his face. When they arrived at her cabin, he saw her safely inside.

"Thank you, Mr. Harrington," Betsy said to him from the doorway, having finally gathered enough air to speak.

Adam shook his head. "I've never liked him. He's a greedy deadbeat—wants a lot of pay for not much effort—but I never thought he'd stoop so low as to manhandle a girl. Tell your ma and pa."

She nodded. "I will."

Later, after much discussion with her parents, she lay awake in bed for some time. The room held only a small amount of light from the sliver of a moon outside, so she stared up into near-black darkness, listening to the crickets and thinking about the evening's events.

Her parents had been furious to hear that Johnny had spoken to her in such a way and bruised her arm, and they were pleased to learn that Adam had fired him. Her pa had shaken his head and said, "I always think he's too hard on the hands, but right about now I'm feeling grateful he's a hard case."

Betsy was more convinced than ever that she didn't want to marry a cowboy. She determined while lying in bed rubbing her arm that she would indeed place an order in the paper for a mail-order groom. But she needed to go about it without anyone knowing. Her parents wouldn't approve. If she told them, they would scold her and insist that she marry someone in town.

She shuddered at the memory of Johnny spitting on the ground and his comparison of her to a female dog. She didn't want to settle for ill-mannered boys her own age. She wanted a gentleman, someone older and more mature, who would treat her like a lady. Before she drifted to sleep, the matter was settled in her mind. She would post an ad in the paper for a husband, just like Susannah had done, and hope she'd be as lucky in finding one.

A few days later, when she walked to the telegraph office to send her advertisement to the New York paper, she felt a stab of guilt over what she was about to do. She'd never done anything secret before, and now she was engaging in a clandestine activity of great importance. Not only that, she'd decided to stretch the truth about her age in the advertisement. Since she wanted an older man, one who was mature unlike the boys she knew in town, she decided she would need to present herself as a little older.

She gave her advertisement one final read-through before handing it to the clerk.

Woman, fair of face and strong of body, 25, seeks man age 25 to 35, for marriage. Must be well-dressed and well-mannered. Occupation of a gentleman required. Skills in music and dancing preferred. Respond to Betsy Blake of Virginia City, Nevada.

Satisfied, she left the telegraph office and walked to the post office, where she informed the postmaster of the letters she anticipated receiving from men responding to her ad. She asked for his silence, and he agreed when she handed him the money she'd earned from watching Caleb and Mini.

As she trotted home, she felt guilty again, both for not telling her parents of her plan and for lying about her age. She justified the misdeeds in her mind, however, with the knowledge that her parents would likely be happy in the end to see her married to a gentleman.

As for her future husband, she would explain the reason for lying about her age when she met him. Surely he would understand she was only putting measures in place to ensure their compatibility. Since she acted older than her eighteen years, she didn't want to be matched up with someone any younger than twenty-five.

She arrived at the cabin after her errand in town to find that both her parents were away, her pa at the range working and her ma likely in the barn feeding the horses. She walked to her room. As soon as she entered, she immediately knew something wasn't right. Perusing the space, her heart began to pound painfully in her chest.

It took a few moments to realize that everything was different, but only slightly. The rug over the hardwood floor was bunched up in one spot, revealing a lighter, cleaner portion of the floor. Her dresser had been moved, only a few inches, but enough that she noticed the skewing of her reflection in the mirror on top of it. The top drawer containing her undergarments was open, and when she looked inside, she saw that someone had rummaged through them, leaving them unfolded and scattered.

The changes felt insidious and taunting, and she suspected who they came from. Johnny was letting her know that he had been there. She felt unnerved, but what she found on her pillow terrified her. Her hands trembled as she picked up the folded piece of paper and opened it. Attached to the note was a dead butterfly, speared through the middle with a pin. Upon reading the message, scrawled in red ink, she dropped the letter and ran out of the house.

Dearest Betsy, aren't butterflies beautiful? You remind me of a butterfly. Did you know that if you kill one, it can't fly away from you? Its beauty can be admired forever.

Chapter Two

Roderick Mason watched Annabelle storm out of the restaurant in tears. He rubbed the spot on his cheek where she'd slapped him and looked around to see the other patrons in the New York Steakhouse shaking their heads in disapproval at him.

Nosy old biddies, he grumbled to himself.

He had a reputation for being a bit of a rascal and had been slapped by offended women before. Still, it never failed to surprise him when it happened, and especially this time. Annabelle was a picture of grace and manners. Truth be told, he admired the fact that she'd walloped him and wished she'd exhibited that much pluck earlier on in their acquaintance. Instead, she'd always acted as steady and as emotionless as a rock. Like most women of her station, she kept her voice perfectly soft and level and batted her eyes in such a way that made most men's legs turn to jelly.

If Roderick were like most men, that day he'd have asked for the beautiful Annabelle's hand in marriage at the fine dining establishment. They'd been courting for three months and that was more than enough time to preface an engagement. Instead, he'd decided to act so appallingly that she would end the courtship altogether. He knew it was better for a woman's pride if she did the breaking up, and he felt he owed her that bit of dignity as a parting gift.

That was why, as he poured her tea, he explained in graphic detail his various sexual proclivities or, as those in polite society would call them, deviances. It was his description of figging that finally incited the reaction he was waiting for. He told her how he would like to bare her bottom, bend her over the bed, and stick a freshly skinned finger of ginger up her bottom hole. Annabelle's eyes had widened considerably, and her cheeks assumed a rather fetching pink quality. He went on to explain the effects doing so would have on her lovely posterior, more specifically the burning that would spread throughout her anus and warm her entire nether region. He said it would be an effective punishment for her, should she ever behave poorly while they were married.

It was at that point that she stood from her chair and exclaimed, "You unwholesome miscreant! I've never heard anything so disgusting and unnatural. You deserve to be tied to the whipping post and flogged!"

Without changing his expression, he set down the pot of tea and held out the sugar to her, which she ignored. He shrugged and set it down. "Funny you should mention that, darling," he responded smoothly. I rather like the idea of flogging. Flogging you, that is. Not me."

At that point she told him she never wanted to see him again and slapped him across the face. He saw stars for a moment, but recovered quickly enough. His mission complete, he drew a deep breath and leaned back in his chair.

"Done with your meal, sir?" the waiter asked stiffly, looking down his long nose at Roderick with what was clearly disapproval. He'd be the gossip of the city for weeks—the scamp who made the lovely Annabelle Jones cry.

"Yes, thank you," Roderick replied, placing the knife and fork neatly across the plate. "I will have a cup of coffee now, if you please." He flashed a wink and a smile at the group of older ladies sitting at a table nearby, who were quite obviously whispering about him. They probably assumed he would leave the diner after being so publicly shamed, but Roderick refused to behave in any way predictable to those who judged him.

Society and its wretched predictability could go to blazes. That was, in fact, his main problem with Annabelle. She was perfectly lovely and observed every etiquette with practice and ease, from daintily dabbing at her brow with her embroidered handkerchief to treating him to a quaint ditty on the piano. Everything she did bored him. There was nothing exciting or unique about their communication, for she would never dare to say something unseemly in order to make him laugh. Her words were spoken with care and feminine coquettishness. If he married her, he could pretty much guess how the rest of his life would go.

Their wedding would be an extravagant event worthy of two society people in New York. She would probably sing a popular love song and dedicate it to him with a shy smile. She knew music just well enough to be considered good, just like she knew enough French, embroidery, and painting. Nothing about her was extraordinary, except perhaps her impressive ability to be ordinary in everything.

They would have children, two probably, and their children would grow up in a way suitable to people of their station. A nanny would see to most of their care, while Annabelle would attend to the duties expected of her: hosting dinner parties, attending charities, and visiting acquaintances. He would spend his free time, when he wasn't working as an architect at the most successful firm in the city, hunting and playing polo.

All would be perfectly nice. The problem was that Roderick couldn't imagine anything more loathsome than having a nice life. He wanted adventure, and he wanted a woman who challenged him, not one who fit nicely into his life.

He felt a pang of guilt for his ungenerous thoughts toward Annabelle. She wasn't the right woman for him, but she wasn't a horrible person either and she didn't deserve such contempt. Ending the courtship was a blessing for both of them. Though she clearly hated him now and likely felt hurt, in the long run he'd done her a favor. It would be hell for her, being married to a husband with such an impossible itch that needed scratching.

Roderick felt something not quite as serious as despair, but more painful than disappointment. He didn't see how he would ever find what he wanted. He wanted a woman without airs or devices, someone as guileless as a child and as outspoken as a man. Did such a woman exist? Sipping his coffee, he picked up the newspaper and read it as a way to distract himself. He turned to the personals section that contained ads written by single men in the west, which was always interesting reading for him. It provided a glimpse into a totally different lifestyle than he knew.

The west held a sort of intrigue to many in the east. Like others in his circle, he enjoyed reading about matters foreign to him, such as ranching and farming. More than once he'd thought about traveling there and seeing what all the fuss was about.

As he read the ads, something caught his attention. He squinted, unsure if he'd read correctly. Nestled between two men's ads was an ad written by a lady requesting a groom. That was certainly different. It seemed she wanted someone mannerly and well dressed, who was a gentleman. His lips quirked up. Silly girl. She probably thought all men in the east strutted around in tailcoats and top hats. Of course, he was not much better enlightened about women in the west. He pictured them all wearing gingham, bonnets, and bows that were twenty years out of fashion.

As Roderick savored every word of the unique advertisement, he came to realize that he possessed every preferred and required trait the young lady was seeking. He thought about how much more he could impress her, if she was indeed so unfamiliar with a gentleman's behavior, and he wondered how many men would respond to her. Would she receive any legitimate responses at all?

She offered nothing in return to a man moving out west to court her, unlike the men's ads which promised their bride security and a place to live. The only kind of men who might venture in Betsy Blake's direction were men such as himself, who had very little to lose and who possessed the means in which to take a trip for pleasure. He doubted there were many men like him at all. A grim realization hit him. She might very well become a victim of a man with ill intentions, who would enjoy toying with a woman naive enough to boldly place a foot into unknown territory.

Roderick didn't even know her, but that thought infuriated him. He admired what she was trying to do and, perhaps more significant, he understood it. She was trying to find someone well-suited for her, and she was willing to take a risk in order to do so. That was much braver than anything he'd done to find a spouse. He'd only courted the women he was supposed to associate with according to everyone's expectations around him.

He gulped down the rest of his coffee. Before he could overthink it, he strode to the telegraph office and sent Miss Betsy Blake a response.

Man, 30, architect by trade, in want of a strong, fair-faced young lady. Knows manners and etiquette. Can even dance and play the piano in exchange for a smile. Respond to Roderick Mason of New York City.

It was a flippant-sounding note, written hurriedly without much thought because he knew he'd likely not receive a response. As soon as he wrote and sent it, he pushed the matter out of his mind, not wanting to get his hopes up and feeling rather silly for having any hopes at all.

He continued on with the activities of his life, feeling dull and uninspired, and on top of that displeased with himself for not being appreciative of his good fortune. He often wondered if there was a God looking down on him, mourning the fact that all the blessings he bestowed on one man were in no way returned with gratitude.

Roderick had achieved great success as an architect in New York City, having created original plans for beautiful buildings that were praised by architects throughout the country and abroad. His reason for going into architecture, besides having a knack for design, was because he liked studying buildings. That had been a source of pleasure for him, from as far back as he could remember. He especially like studying the various structures of houses, and he supposed that had something to do with never having a place to call home as a child. His parents died when he was very young, and though they left him with a generous inheritance, he effectively grew up in boarding school.

Now as an adult, he enjoyed owning his own house, which he'd designed. An attachment to it formed, since it was the first place he'd ever felt comfortable and settled into. The modern touches he gave the building served as symbols of his talent, but otherwise he did not like to flaunt his skills. He'd kept his architectural awards in a stack on his desk until his butler insisted on hanging them in the corridor next to the paintings of his deceased mother and father. It wasn't that he didn't take pride in his accomplishments, but he didn't put much weight on them. They didn't seem all that extraordinary to him, for he hadn't achieved what he considered the most valuable and impressive accomplishment of all—love and a family to share his wealth with.

When his butler delivered a letter from Miss Blake to him in his study on a cold September morning, Roderick couldn't contain his excitement. He set aside his tobacco pipe, grasped the envelope, and tore it open, eager to see what it held. He hadn't experienced that kind of curiosity since childhood.

His heart leapt at first glance of the letter. It was two pages long and written in penmanship he would describe as sweet, with shorter strokes than someone on his side of the country would use. To his great pleasure, the letter was well-written with no obvious errors, even as it conveyed a sort of charming innocence flowing from the hand that wrote it.

I was delighted, sir, to read your telegram. Yours was the only note that made me laugh, and I thought that if you could make me laugh from thousands of miles away, in person you are likely to be a true merrymaker.

On it went, praising him for having manners and being able to dance. It was preposterous, but Roderick puffed up with pride at this stranger's frank appreciation of his trifling note. Toward the end of the letter, she explained that she was the daughter of a ranch foreman, who everyone thought should marry a cowboy, but she wanted someone different from the rough-edged men around town, and that was why she had written an ad in the paper.

This pleased Roderick greatly, as he shared her desire for a new and exciting romance. He moved to his desk and penned a response, similar in length, telling her about himself and his interests. He told her that he too was looking for a different sort of woman than those in his neighborhood and that he was most impressed by her plain and honest communication with him. He finished the letter by making clear his intentions.

At the risk of sounding too forward, Miss Blake, I would like to make your acquaintance sooner rather than later. Provided that you respond to my wish favorably, I shall summarily set out for the west.

Awaiting your reply with much anticipation. Yours truly,

Roderick Mason

***

Six months later

The train screeched to a halt at the Virginia City stop. Roderick had never been so glad to arrive anywhere as he did at that station. It had been a long, arduous journey of more than two thousand miles, some of it by stagecoach, most by train, that in its entirety took nearly a month. He peered out the window, looking for a woman with long, dark hair, as Betsy had described herself in her second of three letters to him. His eyes fell on someone of her appearance, looking wide-eyed and terribly nervous, and he knew without a doubt it was her. He smiled as he observed her sweet flushed face and slender but womanly figure. She was even more beautiful than he'd imagined.

He stood with the other passengers. A weary but positive hum of voices surrounded him. All were relieved to be at Virginia City. For some, like him, it was their final destination. Others would enjoy a chance to stretch their legs before boarding again and heading to California. Roderick took quick inventory of his clothes and brushed off some lint from his trousers. Everything he wore was brand new. His shirt was crisp white under a black leather vest, a casual look made slightly more formal by the western-style tie around his neck that he'd never worn before that day.

He hoped he didn't appear like too much of a greenhorn. He wanted to blend in with the other men, but he also wanted to stand out enough that Betsy would be impressed by him. Never before had he felt so nervous and excited as he did while walking to the front exit of the train. It struck him that he'd never before been nervous to meet a woman, no matter her status, but now a sweet little country girl was setting his heart a-racing.

Roderick stepped down to the platform and gave the porter a dollar to fetch his luggage. Betsy was staring straight at him with her mouth slightly agape. After gathering his courage, he removed his hat and walked toward her, his boots clicking against the wood of the platform. Her eyes grew wider the closer he got. What struck him immediately upon reaching her was how young and wholesome she looked. She wore a modest, light-blue satin dress. Tied about her slim waist was a navy-blue sash. Her dark hair was neatly plaited in one long braid that fell forward over her left shoulder.

"Miss Betsy Blake?" Roderick asked.

She closed her mouth, gulped, and nodded, then opened her mouth as though to speak, but no words came out. Her nervousness endeared her to him. The women he'd courted in New York seemed to know immediately all the right words to say to try to charm him. But here was someone who was inexperienced in the art of snagging a man and she'd already managed to charm him, just by being tongue-tied and staring at him with those big, hazel eyes.

My oh my, he would enjoy that wide-eyed expression on her face as he pleasured her body in ways she couldn't dream of. He imagined her on her back with his manhood fully inside of her, stretching her core and claiming her as his as she enjoyed an earth-shattering orgasm. He would be gentle as he deflowered her but, by the end of their lovemaking, there would be no question as to who that pretty little face belonged to.

He pushed his lustful thoughts aside, smiled kindly, and attempted to put her at ease. "I'm Roderick Mason. It's very nice to meet you, Miss Blake."

After a bit more struggling, she found her tongue. She held out a dainty hand and said shyly, "I'm very pleased to meet you too, Roderick."

A zip of pleasure shot through him. *Sweet Jesus! That's her voice?* Roderick didn't think he'd ever heard a voice quite so lovely. It was soft and musical, a slow drawl so different from the clipped speech patterns in New York, and the way she said his name caused a stirring in his trousers. It was very unusual for a woman to speak a man's Christian name upon first meeting him, especially without permission, but her ignorance in that particular etiquette pleased him greatly.

He enclosed her small hand in his. Her delicate, slim fingers and palm fit so neatly in his hand that he didn't want to let it go right away. "Since you're calling me Roderick, might I call you Betsy?"

She blushed. "Y-yes, of course. I'm sorry, I should have asked—"

"Nonsense, Betsy," he said, squeezing her hand before releasing it. "I'm very happy to have you call me by my given name. We are not strangers, after all."

"Thank you," she said softly, her cheeks still pink. She gave him a shy, grateful smile.

It dawned on him suddenly that she was there without a chaperone. Surely her father or a male relative would have wanted to be on the platform with her to ensure her safety upon meeting him?

He cleared his throat. "I would love the pleasure of your company this evening, my dear, after I unpack and refresh myself at the hotel. Might we eat together somewhere?"

A darker blush crept up her cheeks. She fluttered her long, delicate lashes a few times, but unlike the women he'd courted previously, there was no artfulness in the motion. "Mary's Restaurant is open late. W-we could eat there," she suggested.

"That would be just fine, though now I feel like a bit of a scoundrel. I had hoped to make the acquaintance of your father or other chaperone so that I might tell him my intentions and ask permission before courting you. I know it would only be a gesture, since you are of an age to make your own decisions, but it's the courteous thing to do."

A flash of worry crossed her face. She looked down at her feet and swirled the toe of her boot around some sand on the platform.

"Is that not pleasing to you?" Roderick asked, confused by her reaction to something he assumed would be as customary in the west as it was in the east.

"It's just that…." She paused and reluctantly looked at him, blinking rapidly. "My parents are in the next town buying grain and…." She drew a deep breath. "I didn't tell them about my newspaper advertisement or about you coming here."

That news shocked him. Did she not realize how inappropriate it was to meet a man like this, not to mention potentially dangerous?

She must have noticed the censure in his gaze because her worried look deepened. He continued to give her an inquisitive stare, knowing he might appear severe, but he wasn't entirely sure what to do next. She seemed so young and vulnerable, and he felt inclined to set her straight about proper behavior, but it surely wasn't his place. If her father were around, he would discuss the matter with him. Of course, if her father were there, it wouldn't be an issue in the first place.

It turned out that he didn't need to decide what to do next, for Betsy made the decision for him. Her eyes suddenly sparkled with tears. Without saying another word, she grasped her skirts in both hands, turned, and dashed away from him. He watched her flee until she was no longer in sight.

Well, he thought to himself wryly. I wanted challenge and adventure. Looks like I found it.

He wondered if she would return to meet him at Mary's Restaurant in the evening. He guessed not. Later, he would need to figure out where she lived and set out to call on her. By that time, he hoped to have figured out how to approach the matter of her not telling her family about him.

What he wanted to do was turn her over his knee and spank her for that bit of foolishness. He hated to think what might have happened to her if she'd secretly met a man with less-than-honorable intentions. His inclination to discipline her surprised him. He'd engaged in spanking several women in the boudoir, but this was different. His desire to punish her came from another place inside of him, a protective, serious place that had never been stirred so strongly.

Chapter Three

Betsy sprinted as fast as her legs would carry her, all the way to the Harringtons' cabin. She'd been spending most of her time there for several days, ever since her parents had left at Adam's behest to buy grain in the next town. When she burst through the door, huffing and puffing, Susannah jumped to her feet from her chair in the sitting room. "Betsy! Whatever is the matter?"

"Oh, Mrs. Harrington," she panted. "I've done something so foolish." She rushed into Susannah's arms.

Susannah held her tightly. "Good heavens. What happened?"

Betsy only whimpered and breathed hard, clinging to Susannah for comfort.

"Everything will be all right, honey. Just catch your breath a moment." She guided her to a chair. "Sit right here while I get you some tea."

Betsy tried to compose herself as Susannah brewed the tea. By the time she began to sip the warm drink, she'd calmed down and was breathing normally, though she was still overcome with consternation.

"Now," Susannah said, taking a seat next to her. "Tell me what happened."

Betsy explained how she'd secretly posted an advertisement in the paper, thinking it would be a good idea to find a husband in that way, since it had worked out so well for Susannah. Her older friend's expression changed often during Betsy's account of the details, but her most frequent look was one of surprise.

"I met him on the platform, and all of a sudden it became... real. He's so very proper and handsome, everything I want. And I thought to myself, there is no way he could ever want a simple country girl like me. I panicked and ran away."

Susannah leaned back in her chair. "Land's sake, Betsy. Did he come expecting to marry you?"

"I don't know," Betsy said with dismay. "He never asked me, but my advertisement in the paper did say I was looking for a husband. In his first letter to me, he said he wanted to make my acquaintance in person. The two other letters he sent me did not discuss marriage. They only expressed excitement over meeting me and how well he thought we would get along."

A look of relief infused Susannah's features. "All right, that's good. I think it's best to get to know him a little bit and find out what he expects to do here. Did he mention his occupation?"

"Yes," Betsy said, feeling more foolish by the minute. "He's an architect." She'd had to ask her former schoolteacher what that was, since she'd never heard of such a job before reading Roderick's telegram.

"Hm. Don't reckon there's much need for archi tects out here. And your parents know nothing of this?"

She shook her head. "I knew they would disapprove. That's why I didn't say anything." A tear slid down her face.

Susannah reached out and squeezed her hand. "It's a little frightening, I know, but now you must make the best of it. He wants to get to know you, and you ran away without giving him the opportunity."

Betsy looked down. "He looked displeased that my father wasn't escorting me. I couldn't bear to see the disappointment on his face."

"Ah!" Susannah said, releasing her hand and leaning back in her chair. She smiled. "Another good sign. He is a man of honor, if he wishes to speak to your father."

Betsy felt a glimmer of hope over Susannah's approval. "You think so?"

She nodded. "That would be my guess. Since your pa isn't here, I think Adam should take you to town and make sure you're safe when you meet this gentleman again. In fact, I think he'll insist on it. I know he feels protective of you, especially after the incidents with Johnny."

Betsy looked away. Susannah's mention of Johnny caused a shiver to go through her body. No one knew it, but she'd received two more notes from Johnny since the first one left on her pillow. The notes were short but scary. One listed all the places she'd been on that particular day, leaving no doubt that he was following her. The other letter expressed anger, blaming her for him losing his job at the ranch. He said it was her fault he was strapped for cash and the least she could do was spend a few hours with him.

Both notes contained dead butterflies like the first. The butterfly's wings in the second note were ripped, and the butterfly in the third note was missing a wing entirely. Betsy wasn't sure whether including mutilated butterflies was intentional on Johnny's part, or if the damage had happened somehow in transit, but it scared her nonetheless.

She hadn't mentioned these latest notes to the Harringtons or to her parents because she worried that if Johnny found out that she'd told them, he'd harass her even more. He'd already lost his job. Wouldn't he be even angrier if he got in trouble again? She could only hope that if she avoided him for long enough, he'd eventually lose interest and leave her alone.

***

Adam returned home in the late afternoon and listened to Susannah recount Betsy's predicament. His face remained impassive until she explained that Betsy's parents didn't know anything about the advertisement or that the gentleman was in town to court her. He glanced at Betsy with a stern look that made her want to run for the hills once again.

When Susannah finished the story by suggesting that Adam go with her to meet Roderick again, he said with a frown, "I don't know about that, darlin'. Perhaps Betsy should wait until Timothy gets back from Caston. If I had a daughter who did such a thing, I'd want to be around while she got to know the fellow."

Betsy felt very small and ridiculous as the two of them continued the conversation as though she wasn't there.

"We can't just ignore him, Adam," Susannah insisted. "Imagine if you had traveled all the way here, only to be ignored. Timothy and Lou might not be back for a couple weeks yet."

Adam rubbed the beard along his jaw. "I suppose you're right." He reached for the hat he'd just hung on the hook next to the door. Clapping it on his head, he said, "Come along, Betsy. Let's go see your Mr. Mason."

Her heart skipped a beat. "Right now?" she squeaked. "But don't you need to eat supper or something? Rest a little?" She didn't feel ready to face Roderick. Not yet.

But Adam was ready to get down to business. "I can rest and eat in town. I think it might be a good idea to have supper with him, yeah?"

She froze, suddenly remembering something she'd told Roderick. "Oh, dear. I actually… already said I'd have supper with him at Mary's."

"That settles it then." He kissed Susannah's cheek and walked to the front door, which he held open. "Let's go."

Betsy walked past him outside, feeling like a naughty child being led to punishment. She looked back at Susannah, who gave her an encouraging smile. She returned a nervous one.

The one-mile walk to town ended far too quickly for Betsy, who felt more terrified with every step. Of the two, Susannah was certainly the more nurturing one.

Adam provided no words of encouragement or comfort. His face appeared severe, and Betsy worried that she'd disappointed or angered him somehow. Worse, she worried that any negative feelings Adam was having might exist tenfold in Roderick.

"D-do you think he will be upset with me, Mr. Harrington, for running away?" she asked Adam tentatively.

"Perhaps, but I think he will be more upset that no one but you knew about his arrival. You are very young to be drawing up such a scheme."

"I'm eighteen," she said, a bit sullenly.

Adam looked at over at her with a raised brow. "Mm hmm. As I said, very young."

Betsy stopped suddenly. "Oh, no." She moaned and rocked back on her heels, suddenly remembering that she'd lied about her age in her advertisement. Roderick thought she was twenty-five.

"Betsy? What's wrong?"

"Nothing," she said, her lower lip quivering. She couldn't bear to admit to Adam, or Roderick for that matter, that she had lied. "Just nervous, I suppose."

For the first time since learning about Roderick, Adam's severe expression softened. "Chin up. I'd wager that Mr. Mason feels just as nervous as you do."

Adam didn't know her true reason for dismay at that moment, but his words did provide a small measure of comfort nonetheless. She nodded and drew on what little courage she possessed to continue.

They reached the hotel, a green, three-story building near the center of town. "We're here to see Mr. Roderick Mason," Adam told the hotel manager at the front desk. "Do you know if he's in his room?"

The manager, a portly man with spectacles hanging on the edge of his nose, looked up over them at Adam. "Yes, I do believe he is. He checked in earlier and I haven't seen him leave since."

"Which room, please?"

He lowered his voice. "Room 9. Not supposed to say, but I know you. Go up the stairs, turn right."

Adam led the way up the steps, with Betsy following behind, her heart thumping as fast as a nervous rabbit's.

Outside room 9, Adam placed a firm hand on Betsy's back. He must have sensed that she was about to bolt, for his hand on her back served less as comfort and more as a stake keeping her in place. Adam knocked on the door. After what seemed like an eternity, Betsy heard shuffling and then a short time later, Roderick opened the door.

He'd cleaned up, which made him look even handsomer than Betsy remembered. His newly washed dark hair was still damp and slicked back. The distinct smell of pine soap filled Betsy's senses. He wore a clean white shirt not buttoned up the full way, exposing a hard chest with wisps of dark hair. His shirtsleeves were rolled up to his elbows, revealing tanned, muscular forearms.

After a brief look of surprise, he recovered and smiled, first at Adam and then at Betsy. "I'm very happy to see you didn't run too far, Miss Blake."

Betsy let out the breath she was holding, relieved that he didn't appear angry with her or offended. She smiled back. Somehow, she was able to keep her voice from shaking too badly. "I'd like to introduce to you Mr. Harrington. He's the owner of the ranch where my pa works as a foreman. I've just told him and his wife about your arrival, since my parents are not here to meet you."

The men shook hands and expressed pleasure over meeting. Adam's greeting was noticeably less friendly than Roderick's, and his expression still conveyed severity and thinly masked wariness. Betsy attempted to make up for it by being overly friendly. "Shall we dine together at Mary's?" she asked, a little too loudly.

Roderick didn't seem to notice her forced cheerfulness. "I'd be most pleased with that. Allow me to locate my wallet." He patted the pockets of his shirt and then his trousers.

"It'll be my treat," Adam said curtly. "Come along."

"I beg your pardon, but I cannot accept that," Roderick said, looking around the room. "I have traveled a long distance to buy Miss Blake supper, and I won't be denied the pleasure of it now. Ah! There it is." He strode to the dresser and picked up his leather wallet. Stuffing it into the back pocket of his trousers, he joined them outside the room.

While the three of them descended down the stairs, Roderick held out his bent elbow to Betsy. "Take my arm. I won't have you tripping on those lovely skirts."

No such thing would have happened, since Betsy had carefully lifted her skirts with one hand so that they did not touch the ground, but she flushed with pleasure and hooked a hand in Roderick's elbow. As soon as she did, she felt a lot less like a naughty child and much more like a lady. She smiled appreciatively at him, grateful that he had forgiven her for running and seemed interested in picking up where they'd left off. He winked at her when Adam wasn't looking.

During supper, Roderick proved himself to be a charming conversationalist. He told Betsy and Adam about his travels, conveying his inconveniences with good humor. Even Adam, who spent the majority of the time studying Roderick with narrowed, suspicious eyes, cracked a smile a couple of times.

"Anyone want something to drink?" Roderick asked after they finished their meal. "I could use a gin and tonic. Miss Blake? Can I tempt you with some spirits?"

Adam cleared his throat. "Not on my watch. She's much too young."

Roderick tilted his head to the side, seemingly confused by the statement.

Betsy blushed, knowing that Roderick still thought she was twenty-five, not eighteen. "I'll just have a tonic water," she said quickly, before inquiries could be made to bring her age to light.

"Very well. And for you?" Roderick asked Adam.

"Beer, thank you."

Roderick walked to the bar to order the drinks. When he returned, he made a toast. Holding his glass out, he said, "To the wild west and its occupants, which thus far have proved most welcoming." They clinked glasses. Roderick leaned back in his chair in a relaxed pose as Betsy took a generous sip of her tonic. A strong, foreign taste collided with her tongue, and she nearly spit it out, but instead swallowed quickly. The liquid warmed her throat on the way down. She realized it must be gin, and not just a little splash. Her gaze snapped to Roderick, who was studying her, his eyes twinkling devilishly. He gave her another wink on the sly.

With difficulty, she kept herself from laughing out loud. Her delight wasn't only because she felt thrilled to have a real drink, though that was part of it. It was more because she now shared a little secret with Roderick, something that bound them together, and it made her feel wonderfully carefree. Adam seemed none the wiser.

The men argued good-naturedly about the bill, and Roderick won. Betsy couldn't remember a time when any man had won an argument with Adam, even a friendly one, and she once again had to hold back her giggles of delight. She liked Roderick—a lot. Like her, he had a daring, rebellious spirit that others could not easily control.

"This has been a wonderful evening," Roderick said as the three of them walked back to the hotel. "Thank you both for making my introduction to Virginia City so agreeable."

Adam's response was to-the-point. "Glad we could meet. Betsy's pa won't be in town for a few days, and I'm responsible for her. Do you intend to court her?"

A brief look of surprise at the frank question crossed Roderick's face, but he recovered quickly and answered in a friendly manner. "I'd like that very much, assuming she would like me to court her." He turned to her and smiled, a silent question.

"I would," Betsy said, smiling back shyly.

"Very well," Adam said in a clipped voice, sounding like the three of them were engaging in a business transaction. "I'll thank you to entertain yourselves in public. No going off alone together."

Betsy's heart sank. She'd been picturing romantic picnics and long walks with just the two of them. "But Mr. Harrington, surely it wouldn't hurt for us to spend some time conversing without others around," she asked tentatively.

Adam's jaw tightened, and he scowled. "I'm going to insist you follow the guidelines I just expressed, Betsy. When your father returns, it'll no longer be up to me and I assume you'll be freer, since he tends to be lenient. Until then, you'll respect my wishes."

Betsy thought about reminding him how lenient he was with Mini, but decided against it. Adam was strict more often than not, and she worried that any further complaints might cause him to disallow the courtship completely.

Roderick was perfectly amenable to the restriction. "It's a fair request," he said. "It can't hurt, and it will teach us patience."

"I'm pleased that you agree," Adam said. "Betsy is still very young—only just turned eighteen, and I believe you are her first serious suitor. Isn't that right?" He turned an inquisitive look on Betsy.

Betsy's throat closed. She looked at Roderick, who no longer wore his pleasant expression. He appeared confused and then downright irritated.

"Excuse me, did you say eighteen years old?" He looked at Betsy as he asked Adam the question.

"That's right," Adam replied, unaware of the impact of his words.

Betsy stared pleadingly into Roderick's eyes, a silent entreaty for forgiveness over her lie, but Roderick's gaze remained fixed and irritated. Finally breaking the silence, he said in a tight voice, "Thank you again for a delightful evening. I shall call on you soon, Miss Blake." With a short bow, he disappeared inside his hotel room.

"He seems a good fellow," Adam said, as they strolled back to the ranch, oblivious to the silent despair Betsy was feeling in that moment.

She mumbled her agreement.

"He's a long way from home and he sticks out here like a sore thumb, but he has a good humor about it. I regret now that I didn't ask what he plans to do in town. Not much needed here in the way of an architect."

"I will ask him about it when he calls on me," Betsy said absently. *If he calls on me*, she added ruefully to herself. She had a horrible feeling that she'd ruined everything and Roderick would never want to speak to her again.

***

Roderick undressed for bed slowly, mulling over the time he'd spent with Adam and Betsy. It rankled him to learn that Betsy had lied about her age in her advertisement. She'd struck him as a simple, honest young woman, without the artfulness and games that so depressed him about the women in his society circle. But she'd been deceitful with him from the start, it seemed, and he would not tolerate dishonesty. He didn't so much mind her youth, only the fact that she'd lied about it, and he would need to deal with that firmly so it wouldn't be repeated.

Still, he couldn't help but smile when he thought of their time together. She was shy, that was clear, but she was also engaging and interested in learning about him. He too wanted to know everything there was to know about her, for she piqued his interest like no other woman ever had.

The next day, Roderick continued to think about the matter of Betsy's lie as he performed a variety of errands around town. He opened a temporary account at the bank. When the banker, Mr. Taylor, saw the impressive amount of money he was depositing, his posture straightened, and he looked at Roderick with a strange mixture of respect and wariness. Roderick understood. He was likely the richest man in town, and it wouldn't be long before everyone knew it.

As Roderick dined alone in Mary's Restaurant for supper that evening, he got the distinct impression that people were watching him. He knew he stood out, despite trying to assume the dress of Virginia City's menfolk. His shirts were a bit too clean, his posture a bit too straight, and his wallet a bit too thick.

The waitress stopped by his table and poured some lemonade in his glass. "Haven't seen you around these parts," she said. Her accent was familiar.

"No," Roderick said with a polite smile. "I'm new here, and I regret that it's so obvious. How about you?"

She giggled flirtatiously. "I'm from Rochester, New York. Came here as a mail-order bride, but then my groom up and disappeared. Luckily I have family around, some here in Nevada, some in California."

"Ah, that's good. It's nice to meet someone from the other side of the country. You like it here?"

"Oh, yes. The folks are friendly and I didn't leave too much behind in New York. I'd be happy to show you around town if you like. Make you feel more at home."

He swallowed his swill of lemonade. He looked at her, for the first time really, and saw that her lips were painted a deep shade of red. She wasn't a bad-looking woman, but he much preferred Betsy's subtle beauty and shyness.

"Thank you, Miss…"

"Clark. Miss Florence Clark," she supplied, and took the liberty of easing into the chair across from him.

"Thank you, Miss Clark," he said. "But I'm afraid I'm already spoken for." That was a stretch of the truth, of course. He wasn't at all spoken for, but he was smitten with Betsy. More than that, he felt an urge to claim and possess her, and she was the only woman on his mind.

Florence shrugged and stood from the chair. "That's a shame. Do let me know if you change your mind, Mr. Mason." She floated away to another customer.

He noticed belatedly that she knew his name, though he hadn't supplied her with it. Word about his presence in town really was getting around. As for spending time with Miss Clark, he didn't plan to do so. The only plan he had was to resolve the matter of Betsy's lie and move forward with properly courting the young lady.

Chapter Four

For the next couple days, Betsy waited with silent desperation for Roderick to visit. She was so distracted by her hopes for him to call on her, casting constant, furtive glances out the window, that she broke two of Susannah's glasses while washing them. Later, as she walked from the Harringtons' well to the barn to water the horses, she tripped over an exposed tree root, spilling her bucket of water and skinning her arm on the dirt.

Get ahold of yourself, she scolded as she cleaned the wound with a damp cloth. As the hours passed, she became only more distraught. She guessed that by lying she had ruined her chances at being courted by a real gentleman, and the thought of being so close to something only to lose it caused her anguish. If only she could see Roderick and explain her motivation for lying, then perhaps he would still want to court her.

Betsy's parents would be returning soon, and she wondered how she would explain the situation to them, or what exactly would need explaining. It might be over before it had even started and Roderick might very well return to New York City.

In a burst of youthful impulse, Betsy decided she would call on Roderick at his hotel. If she didn't see him soon, she would go mad. She knew visiting him would be going against a couple of well-defined rules. Adam had said Roderick and Betsy weren't to spend time alone together. Besides that, the rules of courtship dictated that a man should call on a woman, not the other way around. Why should she care, though? It also wasn't common for a woman to put an ad in the paper requesting a man, and she'd done that. Didn't it make *more* sense to break the rules in order to set things right?

Betsy didn't want to wear the same dress she wore upon first meeting Roderick, which was her finest, so she wore her second-finest. It was made of satin that *swished* when she walked. Using a beauty tip she learned from reading the *Sears Roebuck Mail Order Catalog*, she ground strawberries in a mortar and pestle, then applied the red stain to her lips. Next she took bits of coal and colored her eyelashes black. She pinched her cheeks and gazed into the mirror. It satisfied her to discover she looked much older and more sophisticated after applying the makeup.

Not wishing to attract curious glances from the townsfolk on her journey to the hotel, she placed a bonnet on her head and dipped it forward to shade her face. Before long, she was standing outside Roderick's hotel room, this time without Adam, and it required all her strength not to run away. She didn't know how she'd bear the humiliation and sadness if he no longer wished to have anything to do with her. She removed her bonnet from her head and smoothed her hair down. After she rapped her knuckles on his door softly, she heard some stirring within the room, which caused her heart to pound.

Roderick swung the door open and appeared in the doorway. His eyebrows shot up. Then a curious, intense gleam entered his eyes as he addressed her. "Betsy," he said, his voice even and low. "To what do I owe this pleasure?"

Betsy wondered if this was something people in the east said, without meaning it. Was he truly pleased about seeing her, or was he only being polite? The look on his face didn't convey displeasure, but neither did he look at her with the courtly indulgence he had during their prior meetings.

"Mr. Mason, I c-came to apologize for lying about my age. I'm s-so very sorry. You haven't called on me and I can only assume that I have so deeply disappointed you that—"

He held up a hand. "Wait a minute, darling." His voice was kind but firm. "I fully intended to call on you after I decided how best to deal with this matter."

She traced the neckline of her dress nervously with her fingertips, waiting for him to say more and wondering what he'd decided to do as far as settling the matter. He didn't speak again right away and instead studied her with a perceptive eye that seemed to pierce straight through her. Despite her makeup and attempts to appear older and more sophisticated, she felt young and foolish in his older, gentlemanly presence.

"It's not proper for you to be here, Betsy," he chided, without any real censure.

Betsy felt she had nothing to lose by being frank at that point, so she didn't hold back her thoughts or try to speak them in a polite way. "You are not one to speak about proper," she retorted. "You served me gin, against the expressed wishes of my chaperone."

A surprised and then an amused look crept into his eyes. "My, my, there's some vim with your vigor, I see. You are quite right." He moved aside. "Come. Let's work out this matter. Properly or not, it shall be solved today."

She lifted her chin in an attempt to convey more courage than she felt and walked into his room. He shut the door behind her and motioned for her to sit on a chair across from his sofa.

"I liked it when you gave me gin, Mr. Mason. It made me feel... I dunno, connected to you in a way."

He sat on his sofa and settled an ankle across his knee. She could smell his pine soap and tobacco, which she breathed in deeply.

Roderick picked up the smoking pipe sitting on the table next to him and puffed on it with a frown. "I thought you were older, and I thought Mr. Harrington was being far too strict with you. It seems to me now, however, that you need someone to be strict with you. It seems like you act as though consequences don't exist."

Hearing his scolding words made her feel ashamed and near tears. She'd never before felt such a desire to please a man, and hearing that he was disappointed in her made her feel wretched. She looked down. "I was wrong to lie. I want to make things right."

"I do too, and we will. Like I said, we will be settling this matter today."

His voice sounded ominous, and she worried that by settling the matter, he meant to say goodbye. "I want you to court me, Roderick," Betsy burst out, then blushed deeply. She peered at him through her lashes, afraid that he might show disgust for her forward remark.

Instead, he smiled. "I am pleased to hear that, Betsy. And I like that you possess little with regard to feminine coyness and are comfortable enough to say that to me. But your lie about your age seems to contradict what I'm witnessing now. Why did you try to deceive men in your advertisement?"

"Because I wanted to be courted by someone older. I don't like the company of men my own age, and I thought that's what I would attract if I told the truth."

"I see."

Why, oh why had she lied? It wasn't like her. "I know you have no reason to believe me, Roderick, but I'm an honest person, normally. It's just… I behave in a manner more mature than my age would suggest."

"I disagree. I think you have behaved not as a mature woman, but as a wayward girl."

She sighed with resignation. "I know it was wrong. I just wanted to meet someone compatible with me."

"Ha!" he laughed. "If compatibility is what you seek, I'm afraid you might be on the wrong track, my dear. We're nearly exact opposites as far as culture and experience go."

She considered that a moment. "Yes, I would agree in part. We are as different as a wolf from a lamb, but just because we're different doesn't mean we're incompatible. Don't two opposites of a magnet cling together?"

He leaned back and drew another puff from his pipe. "Spoken like a woman who is wise beyond her years," he said with a small smile. "But you must know that a wolf generally eats the lamb, so I'm not sure your example is entirely relevant in this instance."

"It's relevant," she insisted. "Just not literal."

"You think so? Then tell me, do you believe me to be the wolf or the lamb, Betsy?" His question was spoken lightheartedly with humor, which lifted Betsy's spirits and gave her hope that he would forgive her. She wanted to make him laugh.

"That depends, Roderick. Are you inclined to bleat?"

His eyes widened before he threw back his head and, much to her pleasure, guffawed heartily. He did not stop laughing for some time, and when he finally did, he wiped tears from his eyes and said, "I rather think it will be you who does the bleating."

"Oh?"

He uncrossed his legs, leaned forward, and stared into her eyes, his gaze now sober. "What I feel inclined to do, Betsy, is to take you over my knee and teach you a painful lesson about honesty. That way, you will know in no uncertain terms my expectation of honesty from you in the future. What say you now?"

She swallowed and studied his dark eyes, which glimmered with intensity that was no longer laced with humor. When she found her voice, she said softly, "I say you are most definitely the wolf, Roderick."

He nodded, holding her gaze. He then straightened and patted his leg. "Come on then, little lamb, and take what you have coming."

His firm words reverberated in her ears and her belly flopped when she looked at his bent knee. *Come on then, little lamb, and take what you have coming.* Her heart started to race. She could hardly believe that *this* was how he intended to rectify matters. Going through the humiliating motion of standing and presenting herself for a spanking seemed impossible. "I... I'm not sure I can."

The expression on Roderick's face was implacable. "You *can*, Betsy. And, more importantly, you *will*. I can see you feel guilty about what you've done. This will be a way for you to feel absolved."

"But can't my apology be enough?" she whined.

"It cannot, my dear," he replied. "Deceit doesn't become you and I never want to experience it from you again, which is why I must ensure you realize there will be consequences if it does happen."

She stared at his hands, which she only just noticed were quite large, and then looked into his eyes. He did not look angry in the least, but he looked very determined. It was hard for her to understand how a man such as this would resort to a physical act of discipline. He seemed too refined for it, somehow. She could imagine an angry cowboy hauling a woman over his lap, but a spanking from the calm, courtly Mr. Roderick Mason didn't make sense.

"I thought... I thought you were sophisticated," she said. "I would not have guessed you'd choose to spank me for punishment."

"Guess again, darling. I'm a man with expectations, an older one at that, and I appreciate your youthful pluck and exuberance, but I also recognize that your behavior could easily get out of control if I do not address it. Be assured that I will not embarrass you unnecessarily by splitting open your drawers at this point and punishing your bare bottom, but it will still be a thorough chastisement."

The thought of one of his large hands touching her bare bottom caused her breath to catch in her throat and her thighs to clench together. Though embarrassed, she was nearly convinced it would be right to obey him and accept discipline. She didn't relish experiencing the humiliation of a spanking, but she did feel somewhat flattered that he wanted to protect her, if only from herself.

She hesitated for too long. Roderick spoke again, more firmly. "I do not intend to be very harsh with you, Betsy, unless you continue to delay. In that case, I will be forced to teach you a lesson about dawdling in addition to honesty. Come now. Last chance for you to lay yourself across my lap of your own accord."

Spurred into action by his words, Betsy stood and moved directly between his spread knees. Awkwardly she knelt down and bent over his leg. His palm pressed gently against her back, pushing her forward slightly to position her bottom higher in the air. The satin of her skirts whispered of their movement as Roderick lifted and placed them over her back. She imagined what he must be seeing—her new white drawers which thinly covered the slopes of her buttocks. He lifted her legs to be positioned over both of his. His hand slid over her bottom and down to her upper thighs where it rested. "My, you are lovely," he said, seemingly more to himself than to her.

Despite her current predicament, his comment made her feel happy. She was glad he found the back side of her body lovely and longed for him to caress her.

"All right, darling, let's go over why you're about to be disciplined."

She groaned and clenched her thighs together, feeling beyond embarrassed and also oddly excited. "Must we?" She was keenly aware of his hand on her thigh, and she'd never felt a man's hand so intimately on her person. Her belly quivered with anticipation.

"I'm afraid we must. There's no use being spanked if you do not think of the reasons for it during the discomfort. The point of punishment is to modify how you behave going forward."

She couldn't help herself. In a fit of rebellion, she kicked up a leg and grunted, to which Roderick responded with a smart slap across her bottom. "I expect you to have a respectful attitude and take what I'm saying seriously, young lady."

"I'm sorry," she squeaked, surprised at how much force he'd put into a single spank. "It's just I'm rather embarrassed about all this."

Roderick rubbed her bottom where he'd just spanked it, causing a tingling between her legs. "A little embarrassment is to be expected, but it's no excuse for misbehavior, just like there's no excuse for lying about your age, is there?"

She felt chastened and shook her head, mumbling to herself.

He didn't find the mumbling acceptable. He leaned forward. "What was that? Speak your answer clearly."

"No, there's no excuse," she said mournfully.

"And do you think you deserve this punishment, little lamb?"

"Yes," she whispered.

"Very well. You will be punished for the lie and then it will be forgotten. We will carry on with our courtship."

Before she could rejoice over that bit of news, his hand fell, briskly and without pause, over and over. The slaps on her tender bottom echoed in the room. The sharpness of each swat caused her to wince, and before long the heat on her backside built to an uncomfortable level. When she didn't think she could bear it anymore, she cried out for mercy.

"Please, Roderick. I have learned my lesson." She twisted against his grip around her waist, but he held her in place and kept spanking.

"Now that the punishment is causing you pain, Betsy, it's doing exactly as it's supposed to do, which is act as a deterrent to future bad behavior," he stated, filling the gaps between his words with hard swats to make his point.

She fell into silence except for short gasps and whimpers when the sharp swats would cause an extreme burning on her posterior. She wanted to take her punishment as stoically as possible, to show Roderick that she was willing to endure such a thing because of her strong wish for him to court her, but it was difficult.

"Will you be honest with me in the future?" he asked, punctuating his question with a hard smack.

"Yes, sir!" she cried out. "Please…"

He spanked her a few more times. Finally his hand settled and soothed her aching globes in gentle circular caresses. "Have I made my point well enough?"

"You have," she said with a little whimper. He continued to caress her until her bottom only stung slightly. Soon the sting disappeared entirely, replaced by a warmth that spread throughout her body.

"You're a good girl," he said. "Though from the moment I met you, I knew you would be a challenge."

"You did?"

"Mm hmm. When you met me on the platform and conveyed that writing an advertisement for a husband was a scheme kept secret from your parents, I felt compelled to turn you over my knee right then and there. I've always liked the act of spanking a beautiful backside, but I've never felt like disciplining a woman."

She looked back at him over her shoulder. "I suppose I'm special, then?"

He grinned. "I'll say." He guided her to sit on his lap and wrapped his arms around her waist. "Now, darling, I want you to be honest with me, and I promise to be honest with you. I will start by telling you something from the heart that is the complete truth."

Betsy had never felt so many nervous, romantic feelings before. Intermixed with the aftereffects of discipline, she felt disarmed and vulnerable in his arms.

"What do you want to tell me?" she asked softly.

"Back home, I courted many women but would lose interest. It never felt real. It felt like each one was playing a sort of game to try to woo me, and I didn't have patience for it. They never surprised me. It was all as expected."

"But I surprise you?" she asked hopefully.

"Very much so. You surprise me with your courage and candor, and you also worry me a bit. For instance, I'm very glad you came to see me today, but you disobeyed Mr. Harrington, and that shows me you have little regard for rules that are in place for your safety."

"He's too strict. Even my father thinks so."

Roderick nodded. "I can relate with your rebellion, as I too find many societal mores restrictive and unnecessary, but there are certain rules that must be adhered to. The important thing is to know when it's acceptable to break a rule and when it's not."

She nodded. "I understand, Roderick, and I'll follow the rules from now on if you want me to."

"Good, darling. I think that's wise, and I want to help with that. I would feel honored to be the one to protect and take care of you. Will you let me do that?"

She nodded, feeling flattered that the handsome man holding her seemed to think she was something special, not merely a plain country girl, which was how she normally felt. She hoped he wouldn't change his mind about that, but even as she sat there on his lap, feeling cherished by her new beau, she worried that he would soon discover she wasn't really all that interesting at all.

Chapter Five

For the next few days, Roderick experienced a chaste but thrilling courtship with Betsy—in public, as Mr. Harrington had insisted. Roderick adored everything about her. She wore her thoughts and feelings on her face, and he loved teasing and complimenting her to make her blush. The way she looked at him with utter awe and adoration when he talked about his job or the parties he used to attend caused a tugging in his heart that was almost painful. She was so unspoiled by the world, so very fragile and impressionable.

Her beauty was unlike any other's. To Roderick, she was a rarity, something to be cherished and kept safe. He couldn't wait to marry her, but he'd already decided he would wait one month, a respectable amount of time, and then make her his. In the meantime, he felt content just spending time in her presence.

When he heard about a barn dance taking place in town, he knew that would be an excellent date for them. Betsy had indicated in her advertisement that she wanted a man who could dance, and Roderick wasn't a bad dancer. He wanted to fulfill her every desire.

Many of the townsfolk attended the event, whether they liked to dance or not, including Adam and Susannah. Roderick danced with Betsy for most of the evening, loving the way her warm body pressed against his. Occasionally they would switch partners, just to be sociable, but when they returned to each other's embrace, that was when Betsy's smile would be a little brighter, her step a little lighter. He felt the same happiness and loved her sweet, innocent touch on his chest and graceful movement on the dance floor.

When Florence Clark appeared toward the end of the evening and suggested he dance with her, he did so only out of neighborly obligation, nothing more. He didn't want to appear like he was ignoring all others in town, especially if he planned to stay there for any length of time.

While he danced with Florence, he spotted Betsy sitting on a bench against the wall, speaking with a man who stood next to her. Right away he could see from the way she was leaning away from him that she wasn't interested in the conversation. He couldn't quite decipher the look on her face from the distance, but when his dance with Florence brought him closer, he read something in her wide eyes that alarmed him. Fear. Luckily the dance ended then, or else he would have had to make a scene of leaving it early. He bowed to Florence quickly and turned to go toward where he'd seen Betsy. However, in the split second he'd turned his gaze away from her to finish the dance, she'd left.

A quick walk around told him she wasn't anywhere inside, so he strode into the night. A blast of cold air hit him, in striking contrast to the stuffiness of the barn. Something didn't seem right. He saw nothing right away because it was quite dark outside, so he waited for his eyes to adjust and strained his ears in an attempt to hear voices. Relief washed over him when he heard Betsy's sweet drawl coming from the other side of the barn. He hustled in that direction. The sight that met him set his teeth on edge. Betsy stood flush against the barn wall, and the tall man he'd seen her talking with inside towered over her in an aggressive posture. Roderick once again saw the strange look of fear on Betsy's face as he neared.

"I'm sorry, Johnny, I really am," she said softly, speaking in soothing tones, as though trying to talk a beast out of attacking. "But you've got to stop pursuing me. I have a beau and he won't like knowing you're following me."

The man responded with a contemptuous snarl. "Oh, yeah? Where's your dandy beau now? Seems he left your side to be with another lady. I'd never do that to you."

"Leave me be. Please?" she begged, her voice cracking.

"What is it about him, anyway. His money?" he asked, his voice rising in volume. "You know, I would have money too if you hadn't gotten me fired. Cold-hearted bitch!"

Roderick didn't need to hear anything more. He'd never engaged in violence before, but never before had he witnessed a woman he cared about being threatened in such a manner. Without hardly thinking, he came upon them, grabbed the man's arm enough to pivot him in his direction, and landed a hard punch to his face.

The man screamed in outrage and stumbled back before landing on his ass. He clutched his face with both hands as blood escaped through his fingers. Roderick stared down at him with his hands clenched into fists, wanting him to get up so he could hit him again.

"What the hell?" the man cursed. "You broke my nose! We were just talking."

"I didn't like the conversation," Roderick growled. "Get yourself gone from here, directly, before I decide to be even less cordial."

After the man scrambled off, the realization of what Roderick had done sunk in. He shook his hand, the pain from the punch now becoming noticeable to him. He worried that Betsy would be unhappy with him—it wasn't exactly gentlemanly to punch a man— but when he turned to address her, she launched herself into his arms and clung to him tightly. "Thank you. I was so afraid! I've never been so happy to see anyone in my life as I was to see you."

A fresh wave of anger washed over Roderick upon hearing her trembling voice. He wrapped his arms around her and held her close while stroking her hair. After a moment, he took her arms and held her slightly away from him. "Who was that? What happened?"

She let out a breath. "His name's Johnny. He was a ranch hand at the Harringtons' before Mr. Harrington fired him for threatening me. He got it into his head one day that he wanted to court me and hasn't let up. He won't take no for an answer."

"He threatened you?" Roderick asked, horrified.

She shrugged. "Sort of. Some time ago he grabbed my arm and squeezed so hard it left a bruise. Mr. Harrington saw him do it and intervened."

"My God," he replied, disturbed over the news and also regretful that he hadn't hit the bastard again. "When was the last time you saw him?"

"Not for a month or more, but…" She looked down and fidgeted.

"But what, honey?" Roderick prompted.

"He's been sending me notes for months now, leaving them on my pillow when no one is home and saying I'm the only girl for him. That kind of thing. And he moves my furniture. It's strange."

Roderick scowled. "That's more than strange. Why didn't you tell me? This needs to be reported to the authorities."

She nodded. "Yes, you're probably right. I worried that if I reported him, I'd make him even angrier. I thought he would forget about me after some time, but that's not happening."

Roderick released her and ran a hand over his face. The news disturbed him unlike anything else he could remember. If the man hadn't given up after months of stalking, he was most likely dangerous. The thought of him hurting Betsy, which seemed a very real possibility, caused Roderick's blood to boil.

Betsy sighed. "I think I might ask the Harringtons if they would mind leaving the barn dance and escorting me home now. I feel tired."

"Of course. I think that's a good idea. I would walk you home myself, but we know Mr. Harrington is strict about us not being alone together." He had a sudden realization. "Come to think of it, how did you end up outside alone with Johnny?"

She chewed on her bottom lip. The look she gave him was sheepish. "He approached me and asked if I would mind speaking with him in private. He said he wanted to apologize."

"So you willingly left with him?"

She nodded. "It was foolish of me."

"It certainly was. He hurt you once before, and you put yourself in a position to get hurt again?"

"Yeah. I don't know that I would have normally. But I was kinda mad at you."

That news took him aback. "What? Why?"

She shrugged. "I guess I felt like you probably like Florence Clark more than me. She's so sophisticated, you know?"

"No, I don't know," he said gruffly.

"She has her eye on you. She was staring at you the whole night, trying to get your attention, and then she got her wish when you danced with her."

"Well, if that's true, I didn't notice. I only have eyes for you, Betsy Blake, and that's a fact."

She smiled at him. "You're so kind to me."

"Yeah?" he asked, crossing his arms in front of his chest. "We'll see how kind you think I am when I tan your hide for putting yourself in danger, especially for such a silly reason."

It was Betsy's turn to look surprised. "You're not really going to spank me for that, are you?"

He considered it a moment. "I should, but I suppose I'll let it slide this time. Mark my words, though.

You will tell me next time you have a problem, with me or anyone else. No running away from it. And you'll tell me if this Johnny fellow contacts you again."

She nodded. "Yes, I will. I promise."

"Good. And tomorrow we'll report this incident to the marshal and show him the harassing letters. You still have them, right?"

"Yes, I saved them. I don't know why. I hate knowing I have them."

"Well it's a good thing you did save them. It's proof of his harassment. You also need to tell the Harringtons and of course your parents too when they return from out of town."

She sighed. "I suppose. You know if I do that, they won't let me out of their sight."

He took her hand in his and brought it to his lips for a quick kiss. "Darling, I'd rather you suffer that annoyance than get hurt."

She looked at him with warmth. "I'm glad you care about me, Roderick." Slowly, her lips curled up in a grin. "It's funny, you know, now that I think about what just happened. I can't believe you walloped him."

He snorted. "I can't believe it either. It's not something I've done before. I was worried after I hit him that I might have offended you, since I know you want to court a gentleman."

"I want someone opposite of Johnny, but I kind of like that you defended me," she said with a shy smile. "It makes me feel, I don't know..." Her voice trailed off.

"Aroused?" he supplied, cocking an eyebrow comically.

She gasped and then laughed. "You're not very gentlemanly today, Roderick Mason, in more than one way!"

He joined her in laughing, pleased that he had amused her. His comment would have earned him a slap across the face had he been courting someone else. How he adored Betsy. "No, I suppose I'm not. Come along now," he said. "Mr. Harrington will have my hide if he knows we've spent this much time away from the event. You'll stay the night at the Harringtons' cabin, right? I don't like the thought of you sleeping alone at yours."

She assured him she would. After safely handing her off to her friends and promising to call on her the next day, Roderick returned to his room at the hotel and wrote out a report to hand to the marshal about Johnny's harassment of Betsy. After that, he wrote about the confrontation that had occurred that evening between himself and the jilted ranch hand.

The next day Betsy and Roderick delivered the reports to the marshal in the hopes that something could be done. Much to their consternation, the marshal wouldn't help. He told them he couldn't arrest Johnny for his harassment of Betsy. It wasn't against the law to write letters to someone and, furthermore, Johnny hadn't signed them. Without sounding very concerned, he bade them goodbye. "Lock your doors," he called out flippantly as they left the jailhouse.

Chapter Six

Betsy felt giddy and nervous as she sat next to Roderick at the Harringtons' supper table. They were squeezed in tightly, since both Susannah and Adam, plus their two children, were also seated around the table that normally only sat four.

"I received a telegram from your pa, Betsy," Adam said, after swallowing his bite of roast beef. "There was a mix-up over the price of grain, so they'll be staying in Caston a few more days to negotiate."

Betsy was disappointed to hear that news, since she looked forward to introducing her parents to Roderick. She also looked forward to not being subject to Adam's restrictions. She reckoned her pa would be much more permissive when it came to her and Roderick being together.

"Sit up straight, Mini, and eat with your fork," Susannah admonished. The child, who was slouching in her chair next to Adam, had just grabbed a piece of potato and stuffed it into her mouth. "Another roll, Mr. Mason?" Susannah asked, handing him the basket.

"I'd love one. I must say, this is the best supper I've had in a long while. I appreciate you inviting me today, Mrs. Harrington."

Susannah's face lit up over the compliment. She smiled at Betsy. "You've got yourself a charmer, Betsy. Don't let this one get away."

Betsy giggled and blushed when Roderick looked over and winked at her.

"I don't wanna eat the beans," Mini whined.

Everyone ignored her, and Adam spoke to Roderick. "Do you intend to stay here in Nevada, Mr. Mason, or will you be returning to New York at a later date?"

Roderick sawed into his beef. "I'm not sure, to be honest. I enjoy this town and the nice folks in it, like you all, but I have a house in New York City and make a good living as an architect. What was missing in my life there was a family to share it with."

Betsy felt surprised. She had assumed Roderick would stay in Virginia City and that if all worked out between them, they would be married and find somewhere nearby to live. "You might go back to New York?" she asked, her pitch higher than usual.

He looked over at her. "Not without you, darling."

"I... I never thought I'd live anywhere else," Betsy said.

Adam frowned at them from across the table. "You two haven't discussed where you might live if you get hitched? That seems like an important conversation to have before you take things further."

"Pa, I don't want my beans," Mini said again, tugging on the arm of his shirt.

Adam continued to ignore her and focused on Betsy and Roderick.

Roderick wiped his mouth with his cloth napkin and addressed Betsy. "Mr. Harrington is right. We should discuss this, and will."

Betsy suddenly had an image of herself strolling down a street in New York City, looking through the shop windows at the various goods on display. She'd always imagined wearing fine clothes and having a life much more glamorous than the one she lived, but before that moment she'd never once considered that she might actually reside anywhere else.

"How is your hotel room, Mr. Mason?" Susannah asked, changing the subject. "I hear it's a nice place to stay and convenient to the various venues around town."

"It's comfortable. I have no complaints, except for perhaps the curtains," he said jokingly. "They are a ghastly color best reserved for sand and straw, wouldn't you agree, Betsy?"

She hadn't noticed the curtains while she was in Roderick's room, being much more focused on him, but she grinned and agreed. "Yes, terrible."

"Wait a minute," Adam said. "How in the tarnation do you know what his curtains look like, Betsy?"

She froze with her fork suspended in the air on the way to her mouth. At the same time, Roderick realized he'd inadvertently said something that would get her in trouble. He groaned. "I'm afraid I spoke too freely. It didn't need mentioning, but Betsy stopped by my room the other day to have a word with me."

Adam set down his knife and fork, and his expression became stern. "I believe I made it clear to you that your courtship is to take place in public."

Betsy stared down at her plate, no longer hungry.

"I'm sure it was just a quick word, Adam," Susannah said, coming to their defense.

Betsy hazarded a glance at him. "Yes, it was a very quick word, Mr. Harrington," she said meekly.

"I don't care if it was a quick word, young lady. You deliberately disobeyed me. You won't be leaving the ranch, nor will you be seeing Mr. Mason again after tonight until your parents come home. Is that clear?"

The news hit her hard. She blinked. "But… that's not fair!" she exclaimed. "Mr. Harrington, please—"

He held up his hand. "It's more than fair. Believe me when I say if you were mine, your punishment would be much worse."

Betsy felt a lump rising in her throat, and her eyes stung with tears. She wished more than ever that her parents were home, but it would still be a few days yet. That seemed like an eternity to be kept sequestered at the ranch, when her first romance was beginning to bloom into love.

"These beans are so yucky!" Mini exclaimed, once again determined to make her feelings about the dish quite clear.

Adam sighed with exasperation and pulled out her chair. He lifted her and set her on the ground. "Go to your room, Mini. We don't say rude things at the table."

"But Pa…"

"Git!" he said sharply, snapping his fingers and pointing at her bedroom. He was obviously in no mood to argue with his child.

Mini's lower lip quivered before she scurried away, just as Betsy's tears were starting to fall.

Susannah scowled at Adam. "You're being unreasonable. These two are just getting to know each other, and their romance isn't conventional. You, of all people, should support and appreciate that."

"What I appreciate is obedience," Adam said firmly. "And I'm not going to sit idly by and allow these two engage in an unsupervised relationship." Looking at Roderick, he said, "You seem like a good man, but we don't know you like we know the men in town, and Betsy knows better than to disobey me."

"I understand your position," Roderick said. "And if I were in your shoes, I'd be inclined to watch over Betsy as well."

"You already *do* feel inclined to watch over me!" she exclaimed, anguished over the situation. "You scared Johnny away when he threatened me. And when I went to your room, you... you punished me for lying about my age in my advertisement. I don't need two men watching over me."

The whole room fell into silence then, until Susannah cleared her throat. "Caleb, sweetheart, go comfort your sister, would you? Your pa hurt her feelings."

"Sure," he said, standing from his seat. He left the table.

Betsy sniffled and wiped her eyes. Roderick reached over and rubbed her back. "Calm down, darling. This isn't the end of the world, having to wait a few days. I'll still be here."

"Let me get this straight, Betsy," Adam said. "When you were alone together at the hotel, Roderick punished you for being dishonest in your advertisement?"

She nodded, now feeling embarrassed in addition to wronged. Susannah and Adam exchanged glances. Was it her imagination, or were they actually *smiling* at each other?

Anger coursed through her. How dare they find it amusing? Adam was ruining her life, and he had the audacity to smile about it? "I'm glad you find it funny," she said angrily, and swiped at the tears on her cheek.

"We're not laughing at you, honey," Susannah said quickly, her expression changing from amused to earnest. "It's only that… well, that's a familiar story to us."

Her words meant nothing, and Betsy sat there feeling miserable and very angry at the Harringtons. She was angry at Adam for obvious reasons, and she wished Susannah had never invited Roderick to supper. What a disaster.

Adam combed his fingers through his hair and leaned back. Susannah shifted in her seat and gave him a pointed look. For reasons Betsy couldn't understand, the whole tone of the room had changed. Adam didn't seem angry in the least anymore, and he finally sighed and relented. "I may have been too hasty to restrict you, Betsy," he said.

She stared at him, confused about why he'd suddenly changed his mind, but hopeful that perhaps he would lift the restriction completely.

Adam turned his attention to Roderick. "I can trust you to protect Betsy's feelings and reputation?"

"Yes, absolutely," Roderick said.

"All right, then," Adam said. "You two may continue with the courtship."

"Oh, thank you, Mr. Harrington!" Betsy exclaimed, overjoyed and relieved at the pronouncement. She didn't understand what had changed his mind, but she didn't need to. She was just happy he had.

Roderick reached over and squeezed her hand. "My impatient little lamb," he said fondly.

Her heart fluttered at his pet name for her, which had only been uttered before during discipline.

Adam shook his head. "Sakes alive, if this is what it's like having a grown-up daughter, I won't survive Mini," he grumbled.

"She'll be worse," Susannah warned. "Betsy has always been a good girl. Mini, well—"

"Hush," Adam said, holding up his hand. "I'm already worried. No need to kill me now. I reckon I still have a few years left to enjoy."

The four of them laughed, and the children emerged from the bedroom, Mini looking quite morose with a pout on her face.

"Poor Mini," Susannah said. "Look at her, Adam. She's not used to you being so sharp with her."

He groaned. "I'm not very popular with the ladies today, am I? Get over here, Mini." When she reached him, he pulled her onto his lap.

"I will eat the yucky beans if you want me to, Pa," she said solemnly.

He chuckled. "Well, that's good of you, sweetheart. No need to eat them today. Are you still hungry?"

She shook her head. "No."

"Not even for pie?"

She blinked at him with wide eyes before she said, "Maybe a little hungry."

Adam grinned and gave her a hug, which caused her pout to disappear entirely.

Chapter Seven

Roderick stopped by the telegraph office and sent a telegram to his butler in New York, explaining that he would be staying in Virginia City indefinitely due to meeting a lady he was smitten with. He asked how all was going at the house. A favorable response came a few days later, stating that all was well and normal. The butler also expressed how happy he was that Roderick had found a woman that piqued his interest. Roderick smiled to himself. His butler had given him a hard time on more than one occasion about his failure to be impressed by perfectly suitable young ladies.

Receiving the telegram from his butler caused a longing for home to enter his heart for the first time since arriving in Virginia City. Though he enjoyed the adventure of the west, he realized he hadn't appreciated his life in New York as much as he should have. It was a life of intellectual pursuit and activities he enjoyed and was familiar with.

Since arriving in Nevada, he'd had to learn tasks which before he'd never had any use for, such as saddling a horse. Though an expert rider, preparing a horse for transport had never been in his purview. It had been up to his groom. Betsy helped him become accustomed to his new life in several ways, including showing him how to groom and saddle the horse he borrowed from Mr. Harrington. Of course, Roderick could afford to pay someone to do these kinds of tasks for him, but he wanted to learn himself. He already stood out in the town, and expecting a groom to prepare his horse for him in exchange for pay wouldn't be regarded favorably.

Roderick still managed to open his wallet frequently. He paid for supper every evening at Mary's Restaurant, usually with Betsy in attendance. To eat at the restaurant every day was customary for a resident of the hotel, but Roderick also ate breakfast and lunch there, unless he was invited to the ranch. Since he didn't know how to make even a simple cup of broth or porridge, he remained reliant on cooks and spent a great deal of money on food alone.

He also insisted on buying Betsy presents. He delighted in the way her eyes lit up upon unwrapping each one. There was something so pure about her excitement, and it never failed to give him pleasure when she would exclaim that she couldn't accept the gifts while simultaneously donning the jewelry or clothing on her person.

Ever since the evening at the Harringtons' when Adam had relaxed his restriction on their courting activities, Roderick and Betsy had spent a great deal of time alone together. He fell in love with her more every day.

Though he'd never experienced true romantic love before, upon it entering his heart, he knew what it was. It couldn't be mistaken for anything else. It was a feeling more intense than anger, yet simultaneously calming. It made him feel like the most powerful man in the world and also the most vulnerable. Every day he would discover something new about Betsy that would make him respect and love her more.

He visited her at the Harringtons' cabin one afternoon while Adam and Susannah were away and she was watching the children. He liked seeing her play hide-and-go-seek with Mini and helping Caleb with his homework. She was naturally nurturing, and it warmed his heart observing what a fine mother she would be someday.

"Miss Betsy, can I go play at the hut?" Mini asked, tugging on her skirts.

The hut, a small playhouse that Adam had built for the children, was just within sight of the cabin. "Sure, Mini, just for a little while. It's sunny, so you should wear your bonnet."

After Betsy tied the bonnet's ribbon into a bow under her chin, Mini bolted for the hut.

Betsy called after her. "We're going to see Mrs. Pierce later, Mini!" She got no response, as the child was already halfway to her playhouse.

"So full of energy, that one," Roderick commented.

"Yes, that's for sure," Betsy agreed. "I can hardly keep up with her. She's stubborn too. I'll bet you a nickel she gives me trouble when I say it's time visit Mrs. Pierce."

"Oh? Mini doesn't like her?"

"Well, it's not that, really. Mrs. Pierce is a little gone up in the head and generally only speaks to herself these days, but the real reason Mini doesn't like going is because she can't go inside her cabin. It's really run down and the Harringtons have been imploring Mrs. Pierce for months to leave it for another empty cabin on their ranch, but she refuses. She's a widow and that cabin is where she and her husband watched all their kids grow up."

Betsy wiped down the table with a wet cloth, cleaning up the mess Mini had just made eating apples and jam. "So anyway, the kids don't mind Mrs. Pierce, but Mr. Harrington has forbidden them from setting foot inside her cabin. He's afraid the roof's going to come down. That means the children have to stay outside. They get bored."

Roderick stared out the window at the vast ranchland. He understood why Mrs. Pierce didn't want to abandon her home. Many people saw a house as just a utilitarian structure, but to him—and to Mrs. Pierce, it seemed—a house meant much more. It held memories and represented security.

"Nothing can be done to fix her cabin?" Roderick asked.

Betsy came to his side and slipped an arm around his waist. He wrapped his around her shoulders. "I think it's pretty run down," she said. "Just an old bundle of logs that probably wasn't constructed well to begin with. The cabin the Harringtons are offering her is much nicer, not to mention less dangerous."

"I see," Roderick said, feeling sympathy for Mrs. Pierce, though he'd never met her.

He continued to stare out the window, deep in thought about his own house in New York. After some time, he became aware of Mini doing a sort of dance next to the hut and yelling. She flapped her arms and ran around in a short circle. *What a strange child*, he thought at first. When she continued to twist and run around, all the while screaming, he grew alarmed, "Betsy? What's Mini doing?"

Betsy gazed out the window lazily. Upon seeing Mini, her face assumed a perplexed expression. She leaned toward the window. "What the blazes?"

"I think something's wrong!" Roderick exclaimed. Without stopping to think what, he ran out the door in Mini's direction, with Betsy quick at his heels. As they came upon her, Mini's cries became louder, and the sound of buzzing filled his ears. Swarming around and stinging the young child was an angry swarm of hornets.

Roderick grabbed Mini into his arms and ran back in the direction of the cabin, getting stung multiple times himself in the process, but nothing compared to what Mini had already endured. The insects were still crawling all over her bare arms and legs, attacking with vengeance. Poor Mini was sobbing and screaming unintelligible words, while Roderick tried to slap them off of her.

Betsy appeared with a torch fire billowing with thick smoke and waved it around her. As they became agitated by the smoke, the hornets soon flew away to avoid it. Roderick carried Mini inside and laid her on the sofa. Fear gripped him. The girl looked swollen to twice her size, and her face was so bloated he couldn't see her eyes.

"What do we do, Betsy?" he asked, panicked. Mini was still screaming, but it was morphing into a feeble moan, and the sound of her anguish drowned out all rational thought from his head.

"I think you should get the doctor in town," Betsy said, her voice urgent. "I'll stay here with her and try to get the swelling down."

Roderick headed for the door. He ran to the barn and saddled a horse faster than he ever had before, silently thanking Betsy for teaching him how. Now that he couldn't hear Mini's cries, he was able to focus. He set out for town at a gallop. He knew that a disturbed hornet's nest was a danger to a full-grown man. To a child, even more so. He tried not to think the worst, but the state of Mini's fragile body and her screams of pain filled his mind.

By the time he returned from town with the doctor, a deathly quiet filled the space around the Harringtons' house. As they hurried to the door, Roderick felt a tightening in his chest. It was too quiet. Belatedly, he wondered if he should have stayed behind in town after sending the doctor. Adam and Susannah were likely at the blacksmith's or the mercantile, but he hadn't thought to fetch them. What if… He tried not to finish his thought as he walked inside.

The doctor rushed to the sofa, where Mini lay, swaddled in strips of clothing from the top of her head to the tips of her toes, with only space open for her eyes, nose, and mouth. Caleb sat on a chair next to the sofa arm, reading out loud from a book, and Betsy knelt in front of her on the floor. She scrambled out of the way when she saw the doctor.

Mud was drizzled over the floor around the sofa and spilled out of a bucket nearby. Betsy walked to Roderick and buried her head against his chest. Her hands wrapped around his back, smearing mud all over his shirt, which he didn't notice until much later.

"You mud-wrapped her?" the doctor asked, though the answer was obvious.

"Yes, as fast as I could." Betsy's voice wavered, and Roderick squeezed her tight against him.

The doctor spoke to Mini in a raised voice. "Hi there, Mini. It's Dr. Edward. Can you hear me, darlin'?"

Mini nodded her head slightly. "Yes, doctor."

A giant whoosh of air left Roderick's lungs. Before that moment, he hadn't been sure if she was dead or alive.

"You did a real good job," the doctor said to Betsy. "She's awake and I'll bet the swelling will go away in no time. I'll just check her heartbeat."

The doctor removed a knife from his bag and cut open the cloth around her chest. He donned his stethoscope and pressed the chestpiece against her heart. The room was silent as they waited for the doctor's verdict.

"Her pulse is normal," he reported after a few minutes. Addressing Mini, he said, "You're a brave girl, and you're going to be just fine."

Her eyes fluttered open. "I don't like mud. It's dirty," she told the doctor in a small, sad voice.

The doctor smiled sympathetically, as did Roderick and Betsy. Caleb took one of her small, swaddled hands in his. "After you get out of the mud, I'll take you fishing, Mini. Would you like that?"

"Yes please, Caleb."

"And I'll give you all my peppermint sticks."

"Peppermint sticks!" the doctor exclaimed in an excited voice, clearly for Mini's benefit. "Now that sounds like the perfect treat for such a brave girl. How about one right now, darlin'? Would you like that?"

"Yes," Mini said, her voice sounding slightly less sad.

Caleb jumped up to retrieve the candy. When he returned, he placed the stick in her mouth and held it steady for her.

The doctor stood and closed his bag. Betsy and Roderick saw him to the door and joined him outside, where his well-trained horse stood patiently next to the hitching post without having been tied. Addressing Betsy, he said, "She'll be fine, thanks to your quick thinking. The mud helps remove the poison from the hornets' stings, and it has soothed her pain as well."

Roderick slipped his arm around Betsy's shoulders and kissed the top of her head. "I'm so proud of you."

After the doctor left, they took comfort in each other's arms a moment before Betsy exclaimed, "Oh! I haven't been able to take Mrs. Pierce her supper. She's probably starving!"

"Yes, how thoughtless of you," Roderick said wryly. "Neglecting Mrs. Pierce in order to save a child's life."

Betsy grinned at him.

He grinned back. "I'd be happy to deliver it, if you like, while you stay here with the children."

Chapter Eight

Betsy accepted his offer to deliver supper, so Roderick headed to Mrs. Pierce's house on the horse he'd previously ridden to town. He reflected on Betsy's ability to know what to do in a crisis situation. She'd always charmed him, but in this instance she had also impressed him. His heart filled with pride that she was his girl. When he thought of his future, he could only see Betsy in it.

Roderick called out his arrival before hitching up his horse. "Hullo, the house!"

A little old lady appeared in the weathered doorframe, and he quickly introduced himself. "Hello, Mrs. Pierce. I'm Roderick Mason, Betsy's beau, and she's been held up so I've been sent to give you this." He held out the basket of food.

She took the basket and invited him inside, mumbling about the weather and how loud the birds chirped in the morning. She seemed only to be talking to herself and not expecting a response, which gave Roderick ample opportunity to observe the structure of the small house. Immediately he saw why the Harringtons wouldn't let anyone inside of it and why they were urging Mrs. Pierce to leave.

The roof bowed downward, looking like it was about to crash in on their heads any moment. The paneling and rafters were cracked and even broken in some places. But Roderick's keen architect eye noticed something that the others hadn't. The reason for the bowing of the roof was simple. When it was originally constructed, holes had been drilled into six places, where a crossbeam and two girders should have gone. He didn't know why they weren't there, though he suspected it had to do with money. A cabin could stand for some time without those expensive reinforcements. As time weathered the wood, however, the support became imperative. Providing it would eliminate the need for Mrs. Pierce to leave the cabin for safety purposes.

Knowing there was such a simple solution raised Roderick's spirits. Later that day, he made quiet plans with the town carpenter, who built the materials needed and installed them inside her house. He paid for the materials and labor, of course, and word got around town about his minor good deed. He would have preferred for no one to make a fuss, but when Betsy found out about it, she acted like he was a hero.

She stopped by his hotel room and wrapped her arms around his waist for a hug, which he returned, enjoying the floral scent that wafted from her hair. Betsy took the liberty to hug him often, which drove him wild. She would innocently press her breasts against his chest and inspire all kinds of wicked thoughts about what he would like to do to her body.

Releasing her hold, she beamed up at him. "You were so kind to do that for Mrs. Pierce. Why didn't you say anything. I could have—"

He held up his hand to stop her. "It was nothing, darling. I've been trained and I have experience in architecture, that's all. What you did with Mini? That was a truly heroic act."

Betsy shook her head emphatically. "The way I see it, you saved Mrs. Pierce's life. I think she might have died of grief if the Harringtons removed her from her house. And I think they were just about to do it for her own safety."

Roderick sighed with mock exasperation. "Fine, we're both heroes. Satisfied?"

She grinned at him. "Mostly. Now can you please be my hero and get rid of Johnny?"

As soon as she said the name, Roderick sobered completely and his mood grew dark. "Why? He hasn't contacted you again, has he?"

Her face clouded as well, looking regretful over having brought it up. She let out a sigh. "Not directly."

"What does that mean, 'not directly'?"

She looked down at her shoes. "He's been in my room again a couple times while I wasn't there. He stole the brooch and shawl you gave me."

Roderick clenched his jaw. "Didn't I say you were to tell me if he bothered you again?"

"Yes," she said, her voice small. She wouldn't look at him, and he watched a pink tinge creep over her cheeks. "I didn't want to tell you because after he stole the brooch, I thought I'd lost it and felt ashamed. But then when the shawl disappeared too I realized what likely happened."

Frustration grew inside of him, and his rage over Johnny daring to set foot inside Betsy's room made him want to punch a wall. He turned and strode to the window to look outside and gather his thoughts and cool his temper. He felt inclined to yell at Betsy, and didn't want to take his anger out on her. She deserved a good scolding for not telling him about Johnny's harassment, but Johnny deserved the brunt of his wrath.

Betsy joined him by the window. "I'm sorry, Roderick. I should have told you."

"Yes, you should have. I can't protect you if I'm not kept apprised of all the facts. We must report these thefts to the marshal."

"But it won't work! There's no proof that he stole the items, and if Johnny finds out we told the marshal, he'll only get angrier!"

Roderick knew she was right. Reporting it would do little good. He would have to think about a better way to solve the matter. In the meantime, there was one thing he would take care of, and that was Betsy's disobedience.

He glared at her and pointed at the sofa. "Go bend yourself over the arm of the sofa. You're getting three licks with my belt for your delay in telling me the latest information about Johnny."

Her eyes widened, and she visibly gulped. "But Roderick, I wasn't sure at first. I didn't want to upset you unnecessarily if I didn't have to."

"That's not how our relationship works, Betsy. Your problems are my problems, and I'd rather be upset than have something happen to you because I wasn't aware of everything going on."

She fidgeted and stared pleadingly into his eyes.

He had no patience for her reticence. "It's five licks now," he said. "Further dawdling will make it ten."

She finally felt compelled to obey and rushed to the sofa. As she bent over it, he removed the belt from around his waist.

He flipped up her skirts, revealing her white drawers, and considered parting them so she would feel the chastisement on her bare skin. He decided against it, however. The licking over her thin underclothes would be painful and enough of a deterrent. He folded the belt in his hand. Without pause, he whipped her five times. She cried out and kicked up both her feet, but did not stand from her bent-over spot on the sofa.

As he put the belt back around his waist, she peered back at him with a watery gaze. "I'm sorry," she said with a whimper. "Forgive me?"

"Of course, darling. Come here."

She lifted herself off the sofa and fell into his embrace. He stroked her hair and held her close, enjoying the feeling of having her safe in his arms for the time being. He wished he could keep her in his arms always.

Ensuring that Betsy would always tell him everything that happened with Johnny was only a fraction of the problem. Johnny shouldn't be contacting her at all, and Roderick decided he would do whatever necessary to prevent it from continuing.

CATCHING BETSY

***

Betsy found out that Roderick had paid Johnny an unfriendly visit the next day while she was feeding the chickens. Her bucket empty, she walked to the barn to fill it with more grain. On top of the sack was a folded letter. Tears immediately stung her eyes. She knew who it was from.

With trembling hands she opened the note. Inside were two pinned butterflies. One was complete, the other broken in half with shredded wings. Written in red were words that brought a new fear into her heart.

Tell him to fly away before he gets caught in my net.

She ran to her horse, slipped a bridle over her head, and rode the horse bareback directly to Roderick's hotel. She took the stairs two at a time, panting. As soon as she saw him appear in the doorway, she flew into his arms, relief overcoming her.

"He's threatening you now!" Betsy cried, breathing hard. "Look at this," she exclaimed, shoving the note into his hands. "What if he hurts you, Roderick? I couldn't bear it!"

Roderick read the note slowly, then folded it and placed it on his dresser. "I know the feeling, darling, as I feel the same about you. But I don't believe I'm the target. He's only trying to scare and intimidate you further with this. You're the subject of his thoughts and the person who's in danger."

"You don't know that for sure," she responded firmly. "This could be a serious threat against you."

"It could be," he admitted. "Who knows how his loony mind is working?" His jaw clenched. "I guess my having words with him yesterday helped absolutely nothing."

"What can we do now, Roderick? It's only getting worse, and now I'm even more scared."

He rubbed his chin. "One thing is to make sure you're safe in your cabin. I don't think he'd be so brazen as to break in at night while your pa is there, but I'm going to hire the carpenter to reinforce your windows and doors."

"But what if he goes after you?"

His eyes slowly turned to stone. "I hope he does. It'll give me an excuse to kill him."

Chapter Nine

Roderick and Betsy continued with their courtship, taking care to remain vigilant for any more signs of Johnny's harassment. Like before, Roderick reported the letter to the marshal and, like before, the marshal said he could do nothing to help them.

Roderick scarcely spent a moment out of Betsy's presence. When he wasn't around, he made sure she was with her parents or the Harringtons for the sake of her safety. As they spent more time together, it grew more difficult for Roderick to keep his desire for her at bay. She was so perfect and innocent, and a primitive part of him wanted to destroy that and show her what it meant to be loved as a woman. Still, he never engaged in anything sexual with her, wanting to protect her reputation as he'd promised Mr. Harrington. He knew that he wanted to marry her, but until it was official, he planned to keep himself from taking her into his arms passionately.

Conversation between them flowed easily, for the most part. The one subject that proved difficult was the place where they would live. Several times Roderick brought up the possibility of them moving to New York together, but Betsy always managed to steer clear of any discussion at length about that topic. He knew the thought of moving was uncomfortable for her, but he didn't realize how much she feared it until the day he proposed.

One of their favorite things to do together was something simple: a picnic. The wide-open space among trees and grass was something Roderick didn't often get to enjoy in the bustling city life, so he made good use of it. They relaxed together one chilly spring day, having just finished eating sandwiches out of a basket that Betsy had packed for them.

Roderick had memorized every word he planned to say to her. He would tell her of his love for her and how she had made him feel alive and complete in a way he'd never felt before. Then he would ask her to marry him and present her with the diamond ring he was keeping in his pocket. Though he was certain she would say yes, he still felt nervous. He wanted to say everything right, and he wanted the moment to be special for her.

Before he could give his speech, however, Betsy plucked a blade of grass from the ground and traced it over his arm, tickling him. He moved his arm away, but she continued to tease him, making his arm feel like ants were crawling all over it.

"You'd better stop that or I won't give you the present I brought today," he warned good-naturedly.

She grinned at him. "You don't like this?" she asked, continuing to slide the grass over his arm.

He tried to slap it away. "No, I certainly don't. It itches."

"I'm sorry," she said, still not making any move to stop. Her eyes danced with glee over the fact that she was bothering him.

"You're a brat, you know."

She nodded. "Yes, I know. And you're a gentleman, too mannerly to stop me." Her voice had a certain challenging quality about it that made him lift his brow. He took the blade of grass out of her hand and tossed it aside.

"If you recall, my being a gentleman won't prevent me from disciplining a deserving brat."

She waved her hand dismissively. "Those spankings barely hurt."

He laughed. "Darling, if you want a session over my knee, you don't need to goad me. You need only ask. I'd be happy to oblige."

"Will you oblige if I ask you to kiss me?"

He coughed a laugh. She never failed to delight him with her candor and cheek. She scooted closer and gazed up at him, her eyes full of pleading that made his heart travel somewhere up near his throat. Her lips looked full and sweet.

"Why haven't you kissed me yet?" she asked. "We've been courting for a whole month."

He smiled. "Is that so long?"

"Yes," she said, a whine in her voice.

"Very well." He leaned down as though to do immediately as she asked, watching her eyes close in anticipation. As soon as she was no longer looking, he took firm hold of her arm and tossed her over his knees.

She yelped in mock indignation as his hand came down in swats on her seat. "This is what happens to impatient little brats. They get spanked," he said.

She giggled gleefully and squirmed, obviously enjoying every bit of the impromptu punishment. "Then kissed?" she inquired hopefully.

He laughed. He couldn't imagine a more delightful creature existed anywhere in the world, and he considered himself very lucky to have found her. After a few more firm swats, he placed her right side up, and in another swift motion laid her on her back on the picnic blanket. He placed one palm on either side of her, leaned down, and kissed her.

It was the most exciting kiss of his life. When his lips first pressed against hers, the world seemed to stop. He heard no sounds, felt nothing other than her supple lips. She was subdued and in awe, which he knew by the way her lips parted and the gasp that followed, giving him opportunity to explore her further. When he deepened the kiss and slid his tongue inside to meet hers, she moaned and wrapped her arms around his neck to pull him closer.

Eventually, he ended the kiss and pulled away slightly. Smiling down at her, he said, "Spanked and kissed—anything else you want, little lamb?"

Her eyes were glazed with desire and she stared at him with such adoration that Roderick would have given her anything she asked for. "You. I want you," she said softly.

He sat down and pulled her into his arms. All of the words he'd planned to say left his mind. Instead, he said what he felt in the moment. "You have me, darling. Forever, if you want. Will you marry me?"

Her hazel eyes sparkled. "Of course I'll marry you, Roderick!"

He kissed her again, and after that he reached into his pocket, drew out the diamond ring, and slipped it onto her finger. "That makes me happier than you'll ever know."

"Believe me, I know. If you feel half as happy as I do, then you're over the moon." She held out her hand and moved it in a slow wave, causing the diamond to sparkle in the late-afternoon sun. It was a very expensive ring, the very best that he could afford. "It's so beautiful. Are you sure you want to marry me, Roderick?"

Her question caught him off-guard. He frowned at her. "Why would you ask something like that? Hasn't my affection for you been obvious from the start?"

She nodded. "Yes, you've been very good to me. Only, I sometimes wonder…" Her voice trailed off.

He hugged her. "What do you wonder, darling?"

A pink blush crept up her cheeks, and her words tumbled out quickly. "I wonder if you will get tired of me and realize you want someone more sophisticated."

"What?" he exclaimed. "That's not going to happen. Besides, I think you're plenty sophisticated."

"You know what I mean, though. I'm a country girl. I look at catalogs and see what the fancy ladies in the big cities wear. I read about the rules for etiquette.

It's a different life here than what you're used to, and the women you're used to are different too."

"Betsy Blake, I could easily worry about the same thing in reverse," he said, his voice stern. "Stand up." He stood and helped her to her feet. Standing to his full height gave him a more authoritative appearance, since he was nearly a foot taller than she was. He frowned down at her. "I'm different from all the men you're used to. I could wonder if you'll get tired of me and decide you want a cowboy."

Understanding seemed to hit her then. "I never thought of it that way. Don't worry, I'll never want anyone other than you, Roderick."

He palmed her face and ran his thumb along the soft skin over her cheekbone. "And I'll never want anyone but you. We're different but compatible, as a wise woman once told me."

She smiled. "I love you so much."

"I love you too, brat." He pulled her into his arms for a hug and held her tight for a moment. Releasing her, he said, "You would fit in just fine in New York. I can already see it now, you becoming the lady of the house and charming everyone with your kindness and wit."

She stared up at him. "What do you mean, lady of the house. You… you want to move back?"

"I think so, yes. I'm used to drawing up designs daily, meeting with potential customers, and spending time in my library researching. I feel a bit idle and useless here, like I've been on vacation and am now ready to get back to work."

"But this is my home. My family. Everything is here." Her eyes flashed with fear that compelled Roderick to comfort her.

"I understand, honey, but I don't know how to make a living here. There's not much use for architects in such a small town."

She pulled away. "You could do something else," she suggested. "You could wrangle cattle for Mr. Harrington. He'd give you a job."

He shook his head. "I'm no cowboy, darling, as you well know."

"Roderick, I don't think I can move away," she said, sounding panicked. "I'm afraid."

He moved forward and took her into his arms, but her body had stiffened. "I would take care of you. I'd help you get accustomed to life there, and we could visit here once a year or so."

She shook herself out of his grasp and took a step back. Her eyes flooded with tears. "Just like you can't fit in here, I wouldn't be able to fit in there. I know it."

"All right, darling. I'm not going to force you into anything. We'll work it out."

But she was past the point of listening to reason. She took another step away and shook her head. Before he could say another word, she turned from him and fled into the thicket of trees on the other side of the clearing. Alarm gripped him. It was already late in the afternoon and he'd always escorted her home before the sun went down, a result of a promise he'd made to her father.

As soon as he recovered from his initial shock, he took off after her. "Betsy, you stop right now!"

She didn't pay him any mind. He lost sight of her several times through the thick trees, which necessitated him stopping and relying on the sounds of her footsteps crackling against the branches on the ground to know her location. She had the distinct advantage of being able to set and know her own path, which caused her to gain distance at first. Roderick struggled to stay on her tail in between dodging bushes and felled logs.

"What's the plan here, Betsy?" he called out, fear of losing her to the forest making him very angry. "This is dangerous, and you can't run from me forever."

"Leave me alone," she screeched back at him, sounding far away.

"Like hell I will!" He continued his pursuit. Though his occupation required little physical labor, he was an excellent runner due to his frequent exercise, and he slowly he began closing in on her.

He was faster, stronger, and more determined to catch her than she was to run away. When she was within his reach, he grabbed her arm and brought them both to a halt. He held onto her firmly but not tight enough to cause pain as she tried to wrench her arm free from him.

"Settle down, Betsy! You could have been hurt or lost out here! What were you thinking, running from me like that?"

They were both breathing hard. Betsy stopped trying to pull away. With tears streaming down her face, she said, "I don't want to talk to you right now."

"That's fine by me. I don't want to do much talking either." He proceeded to walk with her at a quick clip in the direction from which they'd come. It wouldn't do to be trapped in the middle of the forest when dark overcame them.

After some time spent in silence, Betsy seemed to come to the same conclusion about being stuck in the woods overnight. She let out a little wail. "It was foolish of me to run, Roderick."

"I'll say," he growled. He was struggling to get a grip on his temper. He'd never felt so angry and disappointed with Betsy. She'd put herself in real danger, and all because she couldn't handle staying to have a conversation with him.

She knew him. She knew he was reasonable and would listen to her concerns. She knew he would do whatever he could to make her happy. And yet she'd chosen to abandon him for the forest. Worse than his disappointment over her response to their difficult conversation was his dismay over what could have happened if he hadn't caught her before nightfall. He wouldn't have been able to guide them out of the woods without the sun to help.

"I'm sorry," she wailed, stumbling to keep up with his march toward civilization.

Good, he thought. She understood the gravity of what she'd done. That meant he wouldn't need to explain the punishment before he meted it out.

They reached the place where they'd picnicked. He breathed a sigh of relief, even as his mood soured from seeing the place where they'd just shared a moment of pure happiness before it fell apart. Though they were still a fair distance from town, they were within sight of the path leading to Main Street. After that, it was only another mile before reaching the Harringtons' ranch where the Blakes' cabin was located.

Roderick picked up the blanket they'd been relaxing on before and carried it to a large, sloping stone that came up to his thighs and would be waist-high to Betsy. Without a word, he took hold of her arm, led her to the stone, and bent her over it. The soft cushioning of the blanket would prevent her front from being scratched against the rough surface. He had no desire to cause her pain anywhere but on her bottom. That he would tan properly.

She offered no resistance at first, seeming to understand both that it would be of little use and that she was deserving of punishment. He lifted her skirt and petticoat and draped them over her back, bringing to his view the white drawers held to her slender waist by a thin blue ribbon. He placed his hand on her hip, feeling through the fabric to the soft curve of her flesh that rounded over her hip bone. Finding the end of the ribbon, he untied the bow. His other hand palmed her opposite hip. Hooking his thumbs under the waist of the material, he pulled outward, loosening the drawers completely. She gasped, knowing he was about to bare her bottom.

When he released the material, it dropped all the way to her ankles, revealing her unclothed bottom and legs. There was a chill in the air, causing gooseflesh to appear over her white flesh. Her thighs trembled and she let out a sob, clearly humiliated and cold as a result of her undressed state in preparation for punishment.

He didn't like that she was cold, even temporarily, and he considered clothing her again and disciplining her over her skirts. Then he thought about how cold she would have been if she'd been lost for the night in the forest, where temperatures could drop to below freezing. He decided to continue on with the bare-bottomed punishment as planned.

Stepping away, he leaned against a tree with his arms folded in front of his chest, observing her and giving her some time to catch her breath and for his anger to cool. He would be firm, but he didn't want to be too harsh with her. Already she was enduring more punishment than she'd likely ever received, being bent over and exposed in such a compromising position. Her legs were parted to shoulder width, a good stance to receive discipline, and he could see the soft dark curls of her sex peeking between her legs.

"Roderick?" Her voice was meek. She looked back at him over her shoulder but remained in the same position.

"Turn your head forward and be silent, Betsy," he said. She obeyed with a sniffle.

Finally, Roderick pushed himself away from the tree, turned around, and found a young, sturdy branch. Using a knife from the picnic basket, he cut it down. It was about the length of his forearm and the width of his smallest finger. He proceeded to remove the leaves and scrape off the knots. By the end of his whittling, the switch was smooth. He whipped it through the air as he strode the short distance to Betsy, producing a satisfying whistle.

Placing a steadying hand on her back, he tapped the switch on her bottom. "Have you ever had a switching before?"

She shifted on her feet nervously. "Y-yes, when I was a child, but not…" Her voice trailed off.

"Not on your bare bottom," he guessed.

She sniffled and nodded.

"No child deserves a punishment this harsh. But you're a grown woman, and I expect you to act like one. Is running away acting like a grown woman?"

He watched as a shiver caused her body to jerk suddenly. "No," she whispered.

"Quite right. Now, honey, I'm not trying to humiliate you. However, I do believe you deserve to feel the full sting of this punishment, which is most effective on your bare skin. That is why I have undressed you."

"I-I understand," she said with a sob.

"Good. Let this be a lesson to you."

He brought the switch across the center of both cheeks. A split-second later, she emitted a shriek and would have stood from her bent position if it weren't for Roderick's hand on her back pinning her in place. He watched as a single, thin welt appeared on her tender white cheeks.

He wielded the switch three more times in quick succession, leaving three neat stripes from the center of her bottom down to its undercurve.

She screamed so loudly that Roderick considered scolding her for that, but he decided not to. He had plenty of more important scolding to do. "You'll never run away from me again, Betsy. If something I say isn't pleasing to you, I expect you to stay and discuss it with me. Understand?"

"Yes!" she cried.

He whipped her twice more, the lashes now covering spots on her bottom that had already been punished. Her leg flew up and then the other, dancing in place, her distress evident in every movement and sound.

"Worse than your inability to face your fears is the fact that you put yourself in danger. Imagine if it became dark and the temperature dropped significantly."

He applied the switch to her legs for that, landing four stinging marks from the fleshy tops of her thighs to the backs of her knees.

"Oh, Roderick, please!" she screamed, frantic now to wriggle out of his grasp. He wrapped his left arm over her back and with a hand on her opposite hip pulled her flush against his body, immobilizing her further.

He held her a moment, giving her time to come to terms with the punishment he'd inflicted. Her bottom was covered in red stripes, and her thighs bore telltale marks of the switch as well.

"Please no more," she sobbed. "I won't run away again."

"Three more with the switch." He didn't like being so strict with her, but he'd be damned if she acted so foolishly again.

After the last of the whipping, he tossed the switch aside and spanked her with his open hand. She yelped and then wailed as he continued to spank her hot bottom over the stripes, making sure every inch of her misbehaving hind end was red and burning. He spanked her sit spots very hard, then swatted her thighs firmly enough to cause her to run in place.

"Will you be putting yourself in danger or running away from me again?"

"No, sir!" she cried. "I promise."

Landing one final swat on her bottom, he said, "Stand up and pull up your drawers."

She straightened, still crying softly, and slowly reached down to pick up the material around her ankles. After placing the material gingerly over her bottom, she tied the ribbon. She smoothed her skirts down, regaining all of her modesty.

He regarded her as she struggled to find her composure. She wasn't looking at him, instead focusing on the ground and crying. His heart constricted painfully. He'd wanted this day to be perfect for her, and instead she would always remember it as one involving pain and strife. He reached out and pulled her into his arms. She burst into a fresh torrent of tears and clung to him tightly.

He stroked her hair and kissed her forehead and damp cheeks. "Shh. I know I was hard on you, little lamb, but it's because I can't bear the thought of you being in danger. We will work out this matter of location. I love you and only want you happy."

"I'm so sorry," she sobbed. "I ruined everything!"

"No, darling. You didn't. You got scared and reacted badly, that's all. And I should have insisted we have some resolution about where we will live before asking for your hand. That was my mistake."

"I still want to marry you, Roderick," she said, gazing dolefully into his eyes. "I'll move to New York City if I have to."

He sighed. "Thank you, darling." He was glad to hear that, but now that he knew how much she objected to it, he couldn't see himself ever moving back to New

York with her. He'd have to find another solution, though at the moment he couldn't see what it might be.

There were more immediate matters to deal with, so he pushed it out of his mind for the time being. "I want you to calm down now, honey, so I can get you home. We'll work this out later."

She obeyed eventually, her sobs morphing into hiccups and then disappearing completely as he rubbed her back.

The walk to her cabin was spent mostly in quiet contemplation. At one point, Betsy reached over and placed her hand inside his. "I have to tell you something. I was planning on telling you earlier today, but then you proposed and everything else happened."

He gave her hand a squeeze. "What is it?"

"It's Johnny. He came to the house last night."

Roderick stopped dead in his tracks. "What?" His entire body tensed up. He released Betsy's hand and faced her. "Tell me what happened."

She fell into a moment of silence that caused Roderick to nearly bark at her with impatience. When she spoke, it was with fear in her voice. "I heard a rapping on my window in the middle of the night. When I looked outside, I could see the outline of his body, standing there staring in. I got so scared I screamed and fetched my pa, but when he went outside to look for him, he was gone."

Roderick felt overcome with anger. "Goddamn it, Betsy!"

Betsy started.

He immediately felt regretful over his knee-jerk reaction. "I'm sorry, darling. You know I'm not angry at you for this, of course."

She nodded. "Yes, I know. It's nice to know you care about me so much."

"Of course I care about you. I think the proposal was evidence enough of that. And the spanking, for that matter." He grabbed her hand in his and continued to walk toward the cabin. He was quiet for the rest of the way, but his thoughts were anything but. His mind raced, trying to figure out a solution to the various problems that faced them.

Now his primary concern was what to do about Johnny. Even with the latest event, since neither Timothy nor Betsy had seen the face of the man outside, Roderick reckoned Johnny couldn't be charged with something even as minor as trespassing. Realizing the helplessness of the situation angered him. Without some kind of intervention, Roderick didn't imagine that Betsy would ever be free from Johnny's torment or safe from potential violence.

When they reached Betsy's cabin, her parents invited him inside and offered him a glass of whiskey, which he gratefully accepted. Betsy sat next to him, and he wrapped an arm around her, feeling like he never wanted to let her out of his sight after the latest news about Johnny.

"I see you accepted the proposal," Timothy said to his daughter, nodding at her ring.

"Yes," she responded, her face brightening. She looked at Roderick. "You told my pa you were going to propose before you asked me?"

"Of course," he said, relaxing enough to smile back at her.

Lou and Timothy expressed congratulations for their engagement, which brought a happy, carefree tone to the room that Roderick hated to interrupt. But after some time of celebrating had passed, he sobered and addressed Betsy's parents. "I've just learned about Johnny's latest harassment. What should we do about this? Seems the marshal is just shy of useless. I feel we must do something to stop Johnny, with or without the law's help."

Roderick felt Betsy shiver against him. He squeezed her hand and looked over at her. "I won't let anything to happen to you."

Timothy leaned back in his chair. "I've been thinking about this too. I reckon you, me, and Harrington could pay Johnny a visit. Give him a taste of the damage we we'll do if he bothers Betsy again."

"Suits me," Roderick said. By this point, he didn't have any reservations about what would surely be a violent encounter. Before Betsy and before his time in the wild west, he wouldn't have considered dealing with a problem in that manner. But everything had changed, and he felt more compelled to enact justice harshly with someone like Johnny than to try to reason with him.

Lou poured more whiskey into Roderick's glass. It was getting late and there was no moon to guide him to his hotel, but the walk wouldn't be too difficult because of the wide path. There was still another important matter to discuss. He cleared his throat. "Betsy has expressed concerns about moving with me to New York

City, so that's another problem I must find a solution to."

A pained look came into Lou's eyes. "We'd sure miss Betsy if you moved away, but we'll support whatever you decide."

Sighing, he said, "Thank you, but I don't like the idea of causing you all pain, least of all Betsy. I wish I knew an easy solution."

Betsy shook her head. "Don't worry, Roderick. It's not your burden to carry alone. I will adjust, and so will my parents, if we move to New York."

Timothy agreed with Betsy. "I've never seen my daughter so happy. She's found a good man, and that's what's important to us."

Despite those reassurances, Roderick did not feel at ease. For days, he tried to think of a solution, but nothing seemed fitting. He considered that he might take a low-paying job in Virginia City, if one became available, but he didn't like the thought of putting all of his skills and education to waste, especially if there ever came a point in time where he'd need to provide for children. Equally distasteful, however, was dragging Betsy to a totally foreign place she did not wish to be.

His musings about the predicament recurred frequently, and there wasn't anyone around in a similar situation who could give him advice. Even though Adam had come from a different state and successfully settled in Virginia City, he'd left nothing behind and had been ready to start fresh, plus he was a rancher, an occupation that existed in his new town. Contrarily, Roderick had left a great deal behind, and there was no work for him in Virginia City. He couldn't pretend that the first thirty years of his life hadn't existed. He also couldn't see how it was possible to successfully meld his past together with his future with Betsy.

Chapter Ten

Betsy walked with a light step to the seamstress shop. She and Roderick had arranged to meet there to buy her a new pair of boots. She was feeling good about her future with Roderick and about how things were going in general. The three men in her life—Roderick, Adam, and her pa—had paid Johnny a visit, and there hadn't been any more harassing letters or sign of him anywhere since then. She didn't ask what happened in that visit, but she did notice that Roderick's hand was bruised immediately following it.

His fierce protectiveness of her combined with his gentlemanly behavior gave her a sense of calm and general well-being. He was everything she'd ever wanted and more. When he spoke to her in his low, courtly tones, it was all she could do not to melt. Even the punishments, as painful as they had been, were further proof to her that he would always see her to safety.

Her insecurity about not being sophisticated enough for Roderick remained, though that fear gradually subsided. He looked at her like she was the prettiest lady in the world, and that made her feel like perhaps she was exactly what he wanted, just like he was exactly what she wanted.

That was why, when she spotted him conversing with Florence Clark outside the shop, the sudden jealousy that filled her heart hit her unexpectedly. Her mouth became dry and blood rushed to her face. She felt anger and an animal-like instinct to fight for what was hers. She walked in their direction but stayed out of sight. Even when she was within earshot, she stayed behind the shadow of the shop so as not to be seen. She wanted to know what they were talking about before making an appearance.

Florence's plumby voice rang out clearly and felt like nails against a chalkboard to Betsy. "I'm sure my uncle would love to hire a man like you," she cooed. "He's always looking for bright employees, and his business is quite a success. You wouldn't earn as much as if you returned to New York, of course, but it would be a decent wage. I can put in a good word."

"I'd really appreciate that, Miss Clark. Thank you kindly."

"I'd want something in return, of course," she said, her voice sweet and flirtatious.

"Oh? And what might that be?" Roderick asked, sounding equally jovial.

Betsy felt her jaw clench and her hands close into fists. She hated how he sounded like he was enjoying speaking to her.

"You'll have to let me stay in your grand New York house next time I go there for a visit." She reached out and laid a hand on his arm, which he did not try to stop.

Betsy nearly growled. The audacity of the woman, requesting to stay in his house? She was fairly convinced that Roderick would deny that request. Surely it wouldn't be proper to house an unmarried woman.

"I think I can accommodate that," Roderick said, his voice lighthearted. "I sure do appreciate you telling me about your uncle's business. This could be the answer I'm looking for."

Betsy couldn't stand to hear another word. She stormed into sight and walked directly to them, her blood boiling. When Roderick saw her, his face broke into a smile. "Darling!"

She plastered a smile on her face, matching Florence's expression.

"Hello, Miss Blake," Florence said politely.

"Howdy," she drawled, walking to Roderick's side. "I hope I'm not interrupting."

"Not at all," he said, wrapping an arm around her shoulders. "How are you doing today? You're looking lovely."

She was wearing a checkered brown gingham dress with old dusty shoes and a plain black hat. She knew she looked remarkably plain next to Florence, who wore a red satin frock with lace around the sleeves and collar.

"I don't look lovely at all," she retorted hotly, and cast a derisive look at Florence. "Some of us actually have important chores to do during the day. We can't all go around looking like an oversized china doll."

Florence's eyes widened and her cheeks turned slightly pink, much to Betsy's satisfaction.

"Of course," Betsy continued, "there are plenty of benefits to wearing a blinding red dress and bathing in perfume. Good for frightening dogs and small children away, I'm sure."

"My word, Betsy!" Roderick exclaimed.

"I, I will be going then," Florence stammered. "Please excuse me." She blinked rapidly, appearing like she was holding back tears, and then rushed off.

Betsy instantly felt remorse. She hadn't dreamed that she could actually hurt her feelings. It was obvious how much more beautiful Florence was, and Betsy had expected her to fling an insult back, not retreat in sad dignity.

"What in the blazes has gotten into you?" Roderick asked, staring at her with amazement. "I think you offended Miss Clark terribly."

"I don't care!" Betsy exclaimed, though that was a lie. She did care and felt horrible, but she wasn't willing to lose the last shred of her self-respect by admitting that. "She was flirting with you, and you were flirting back." She glared at him and took a step away.

"That's not true," he said, shaking his head. "She was telling me about an employment opportunity that would help both of us. My, but you are a jealous little filly, aren't you?"

Betsy's nose burned and her eyes stung. The thought of Roderick falling for the sophisticated lady from his side of the country caused her unimaginable heartache. The image of him laughing with Florence and her touching his arm flashed through her mind. She thought about her rude words to the woman and how foolish she must have looked, while Florence left looking even more dignified than before by not stooping to her level, instead floating away in her pretty dress.

Betsy then did the only thing she wanted to do in that moment. She needed to get away, to lick her wounds and deal with her shame alone, so she turned and bolted toward home.

"Oh, for Pete's sake!" she heard Roderick exclaim in a fading voice.

She ran, hoping and half-expecting to hear Roderick's footsteps behind her, but when she looked back, she saw him still standing in the same place, watching her retreat with his hands on his hips. Devastated, she ran all the way home and straight into the barn, where she collapsed into a corner and sobbed into her hands. Now she'd really ruined everything. He hadn't even bothered to catch her this time. She cried until she was exhausted and her nose was running. Not caring how unladylike she appeared to the horses, she wiped it on her sleeve.

Time passed, and she made no effort to leave her sad little corner in the barn or even shift positions until she heard a noise. She looked up to find Roderick standing in front of her with crossed arms, staring down at her. He didn't look pleased, but Betsy's heart gave a small leap of joy. He had followed her. He did want to catch her.

"Young lady, I can't believe you went and ran again. Didn't we already discuss you weren't to do that?"

"I needed some time alone to think," she said lamely.

He snorted. "Think? In your state? That's a frightening prospect. What have you been thinking about in that silly head of yours?"

She shrugged a shoulder. "That Florence is prettier than me and you like her more. You think she's a sophisticated lady and I'm a naughty little girl."

He groaned. "You're right about one thing. I do think you're naughty. Naughty and silly and everything I want."

She peered up at him and studied his handsome features. He didn't appear angry, only exasperated.

"Mind if I have a seat?" he asked.

When she made no protest, he sat down next to her in the hay. "This is rather comfortable," he commented.

"It's dirty," she said sullenly. "You're going to get your nice trousers all dusty."

"A little dust never hurt anyone." He wrapped an arm around her and pulled her close, "Now, young lady, what am I going to do with you?"

She breathed in the scent of his pine soap, causing a rush of memories from various times they'd spent together over the last month. In that moment, she knew Roderick loved her more than anything in the world. The scene she'd come upon with him and Florence now seemed perfectly normal and harmless, a neighborly conversation about his occupation. She still believed Florence wouldn't mind if Roderick fancied her, but he didn't. He loved Betsy.

She gazed into his eyes. "Forget this ever happened? Take me to lunch?"

He kissed the tip of her nose. "I could take you to lunch. But if we go back to town, you're apologizing to

Miss Clark for being so rude." His lips twitched. "Over-sized china doll?"

Betsy cringed and looked down. "I don't know where that came from."

"I don't either. That was really something." He removed his arm from around her shoulders and shaded his eyes. When his shoulders started shaking, Betsy realized he was laughing silently. That gave her hope.

"Does this mean you're not angry with me, Roderick?"

When he stopped laughing, he shook his head. "I'm not angry. But I want to resolve this jealousy of yours and prove you're the only girl for me."

She sighed. "I know I am. I just forget sometimes, that's all."

"Then I need to figure out a way to help you remember," he said, a gleam in his eye.

"Like how?"

"I can think of a few ways. How about if we go inside and I show you?"

When she nodded her agreement, Roderick jumped to his feet and held out a hand to help her up. He then bent down and scooped her up over his shoulder like she was a sack of potatoes.

She let out a squeal of surprise but did not protest as he walked her to the cabin. Luckily there was no one around to see her in such an undignified position, since her parents were in town on business. She felt especially grateful for the lack of an audience when he landed a few gratuitous swats on her conveniently upturned bottom.

He crossed the threshold with her still over his shoulder and locked the door. From there he walked to Betsy's room and slid her down onto her back on the bed. "Now, darling, the things I want us to do, they're things done between a man and his wife. We may not be married according to the law, but if we continue, we'll be good as married, far as I'm concerned."

She stared into his eyes and swallowed. "I understand, Roderick," she whispered.

He leaned down and kissed her, then traveled with light pecks across her cheek to her ear, where he said softly, "Tell me now if you want me to stop. If you don't, I'm going to prove that every bit of you is mine, and always will be."

His possessive words and the tickle of his mouth on her ear caused her pulse to skitter. She felt shivers cascading all the way down to her toes.

"Don't stop," she breathed.

His hand slid up her leg under her skirt. "Every inch of you will feel my touch." He loosened the ribbon of her drawers then ran his hand back down to remove her shoes and stockings. He removed her petticoat and shoved up her dress and shift to her waist. The drawers slid down her legs until they reached her feet and were removed completely. "Spread those beautiful legs for me, darling," he said, his voice husky and low.

She parted her knees with a little whimper of embarrassment at having her most intimate body parts exposed. Cool air fanned her nether lips, and the hungry look in Roderick's eye caused warmth to creep up her neck and into her cheeks.

A primitive growl resonated from somewhere in the back of Roderick's throat. He rested his hand on her knee before trailing his fingers slowly along her inner thigh until he reached her aching center. His hand only hovered over her sex, making contact with some of her soft curls but applying no pressure. The feather-light sensation made every nerve ending in her body feel like it might burst into flames.

He touched her belly and trailed his hand further up under her clothes. "Time for that dress to come off," he growled.

It was more an order than a statement. With her knees bent and feet flat on the bed, she arched her pelvis off the bed so that he might push her dress and shift up toward her head and neck. She sat up. The rough fabric of the woolen blanket felt prickly on her bare bottom. He drew the clothing over her head and tossed the material aside.

His gaze lingered on her breasts. They were small with hardened nipples protruding on display. She let out a gasp when he clamped his mouth over one and sucked, flicking his tongue back and forth. His hand found her other breast and kneaded it gently. "God, you're gorgeous," he growled against her skin, kissing along her neck. He kissed her mouth again, this time with a possessiveness she felt at the very center of her being.

When he pulled away and sat next to her on the bed, she let out a whine of protest. "Why did you stop? That, that felt good," she stammered.

"Yes," he said gravely. "I can tell. I want you to feel good and you will, but I would be remiss not to punish you first for running away again."

Her mouth fell open. His chiding words caused her sex to pulse and ache, even as her mind rallied against the punishment. He didn't wait for her agreement or participation in positioning herself for her spanking. Instead he hauled her naked, quivering body over his lap and wrapped a steadying hand around her waist.

"But Roderick, you said you weren't angry with me," she protested.

"I'm not, darling, but you're still getting punished. You must learn," he scolded, bringing his hand down hard on her bare bottom, "that we do not run from problems. We face them together." He spanked her several more times, the swats hard enough to cause a sting right away on her highly sensitized skin.

She yelped and twisted as his hand picked up speed. The spanking echoed loudly against the logs of the cabin.

"And you will also learn," he said while smacking, "who this naughty red bottom belongs to. Who does it belong to?"

"You," she gasped.

"Mm hmm, that's right." The spanking continued, heating her flesh and knocking her mound and sensitive clit against his hard thigh. "And every time you doubt it from here on out, this naughty bottom going to be spanked scarlet. Make no mistake about that."

She moaned, the pain and pleasure of the spanking so intense she needed relief from both. "Please, Roderick!" she cried, unsure of what she was asking for, knowing only that she felt like she might burst.

Her plea didn't move him. "You will accept every earned swat, young lady. We're not stopping for some time." True to his word, he continued to spank her hard, roasting her tender flesh in measured, firm discipline.

She tried to remain still and accept the punishment, but her bottom smarted anew with every swat that layered one over the other. She squirmed, her legs spreading wantonly over his lap as he continued to discipline her. He spanked her thighs, his fingers catching her inner legs as she kicked and spread them. Her belly wiggled frantically against his hard lap, igniting her feeling of helpless arousal and pain.

He stopped and slid his hot hand between her legs, where he cupped her pussy. "This is very naughty, getting wet during discipline. He gave her pussy a sharp spank, sending shockwaves of pain and pleasure throughout her belly and sex. "Are you my naughty girl?"

"Oh, God," she said, trembling with the intensity of her humiliation, which caused unimaginable desire from somewhere deep inside of her.

He spanked her pussy again. "Answer me. Are you my naughty girl?"

"Yes!" she cried, tears coming to her eyes.

"And what do naughty girls get?"

"S-spanked," she stuttered.

"That's right. They get their bottom spanked. And then they get their naughty little pussy spanked and filled." He hauled her forward so that her legs straddled his left thigh. She gasped as he took firm hold of her bottom cheeks and pulled her higher up his leg, rubbing the sensitive folds of her womanhood along the fabric of his trousers. He planted his arm along her back with his elbow at her neck and proceeded to spank her again, alternating between each cheek, driving her pussy down on his leg.

"You'd better not be getting my leg wet with your arousal," he warned. "Otherwise your pussy is going to get spanked again."

She moaned, the threat and humiliation causing a wave of pleasure to build. It grew in intensity, and she felt like she was closing in on something just out of her reach. Her body stiffened. Just another couple swats and she would be there.

He stopped suddenly and rubbed her bottom. "Not yet, your punishment isn't over," he chided.

"Roderick, please, I need…"

"You will get everything you need, all in good time," he said. He lifted her off of him and laid her on her stomach on the bed. "Hmm, it's just as I suspected. Look at what you did, you bad girl."

She looked at him over her shoulder and she felt her eyes widen at seeing the large wet spot on his leg. "I… I didn't mean…"

"What did I say would happen if you left a wet spot?" The corners of his mouth tugged upward, the only sign that he wasn't truly scolding her. His eyes glimmered.

"That I would get-get my…" Her cheeks burned.

He landed a hard spank on her right cheek. "Say it."

"I would get my pussy spanked," she said quickly, the heat in her face intensifying.

"That's right. Get up on your hands and knees, spread your legs open."

With a whimper, she did as instructed. He smacked her bottom again. "Arch your back. Stick your naughty bottom out."

Again she obeyed with a shiver. Her breasts swung down in front of her, and Roderick took advantage of his easy access. He held one gently and pinched her nipple, not very hard. He still wore all his clothes, which somehow added to the vulnerability of her position. Still, she trusted him and all the wonderful, scary feelings he was causing to burst inside of her.

"I'll let you know a secret," his voice rumbled. "I was very happy to see that wet spot." His hand traced lightly down her back and over her hot bottom. "This will be a good punishment for being such a good, dirty little girl."

He placed his hand over her sex and held it there for a moment and then started spanking. Crisp sharp swats layered on top of her nether lips and clitoris, bringing loud yelps and moans. She moved one knee forward, which earned her a hard swat on her inner thigh and a barked order to stay still. He was right, it was a good punishment. She'd never felt anything so shockingly pleasurable in her life.

He stopped spanking her pussy, and she could hear the sound of clothing being removed. He joined her on the bed and cradled her next to him, kissing and pulling her entire body flush against his. His hardness pressed against the apex of her legs. Even though she'd never experienced a man's member inside of her before, she instinctually knew it was exactly what she wanted. She longed to be stretched and filled and possessed.

He moved over her, straddling her hips. As rough as he was with her before, Roderick was gentle as he eased himself into her opening. The walls of pussy expanded around him. After a pinch of pain, he was fully buried in her tight channel. "You all right, darling?" he asked, keeping still.

In answer to his question, she wrapped her arms around his neck and pulled his lips to hers. He kissed her tenderly and slowly pulled his cock through her. Sparks of pleasure zipped through her body. They were so close, so connected. He rocked back down inside of her, the second stroke even more exhilarating than the first.

He picked up speed, filling and spreading her. The buildup of feelings she had before returned, and this time he didn't interrupt. "Good girl," he praised, encouraging her to go to where the pleasure was leading.

"Oh, God, Roderick," she cried, her back arching. Every bit of her stiffened before she jerked in his arms. The pleasure shot through her as her pussy milked his cock, spasming with the rest of her.

He groaned. "You're so fucking beautiful coming for me like that, baby." As the waves of her orgasm receded, his began. He clutched her to his body and let out a growl as he filled her with his seed. The moment he became lost in his own pleasure was a moment Betsy would never forget and would take joy in seeing repeated often. It made her feel like she was the most beautiful, powerful woman in the world that her body could provide him with such pleasure.

He lay down next to her and cuddled her body into his. Their legs and arms entwined like vines. He landed soft kisses all over her face. "My sweet girl. Now do you know I am yours and you are mine?"

She sighed happily. "Yes, Roderick."

As she drifted near to sleep, she recalled the punishment and how it had morphed into unimaginable pleasure. She tried to determine the exact moment the spanking stopped being punishment and began being pleasure, but she couldn't. The feelings were all tied together and led to an emotional contentment in addition to physical gratification. She was Roderick's, forever, and every mark on her body served as proof of that.

Chapter Eleven

Shortly after Betsy and Roderick were joined in the marriage of flesh, they made plans to join in marriage by law. Their plans were delayed, however, because Betsy's parents and the Harringtons admonished them to settle the matter of where they would live before going through with the wedding. Though the two of them were impatient and in love, they heeded the well-intentioned advice.

Roderick's greatest hope was that the position with Florence Clark's uncle at his firm in Sacramento would lead to a secure job that would allow them to plant roots. Its location was close to Virginia City in both distance and culture. He would be able to resume work, and Betsy would feel at home there and be able to visit her family and friends much more often than if they moved all the way to the east coast. As for Roderick's house in New York, he couldn't bear to sell it. He would keep it and maintain the staff's salaries for the time being.

After exchanging a few telegrams with Florence's uncle in California, Roderick was invited for an interview. He promptly bought a train ticket and packed for the trip. He wanted nothing more than to take Betsy with him on his journey, as the thought of not seeing her even for a day pained him, but it wasn't proper for two unmarried people to travel together, so he decided he must travel alone.

The two lovers stood on the platform, waiting for Roderick's train west. "Can you believe it was only a little more than a month ago we met here for the first time?" he mused.

Betsy stood on her tiptoes and wrapped her arms around his neck. "I'm the luckiest girl in the world, having you for a fiancé. Thank you for seeing about this job, Roderick."

He enclosed her body in his arms and kissed her tenderly. "I'd do much more than that for you, Betsy. Anything you wish for, I will do everything in my power to grant."

She sighed happily before her face clouded with sadness at the distant sound of the train's whistle and chug along the tracks. The noise grew nearer, as did the time when they would have to say goodbye.

He swiped a tear off her cheek with his thumb. "None of that. I'll be back before you can miss me."

"Not true. I miss you already," she huffed, her bottom lip protruding.

"You'd better stop pouting. Otherwise, a spanking will be the first order of business upon my return," he teased.

She pouted even more noticeably, which made him laugh. "I'll see you soon, brat." He leaned forward and nipped at her bottom lip, then kissed her passionately, not caring about whether people around them were scandalized. Her kisses felt as important as the air he breathed. He needed them. The train screeched to a halt behind him, and the smell of coal from the engine filled his senses. They clung to each for a final brief moment before letting go.

"I love you!" she called after him as he climbed the steps to the train.

"Love you too, darling."

As Roderick waved to Betsy from a window of the train, a powerful feeling of grief struck him, and he couldn't help but feel like he was losing her. It was entirely irrational, he knew. They would be together again before long, but that didn't lessen the painful feeling.

Throughout the whole of his journey, that same strange feeling of loss would revisit him often. Each time he pushed it away, scolding himself for being so dramatic, and each time it would return.

In spite of the sadness that haunted him, the trip turned out to be successful beyond what he could have hoped. He immediately liked Florence's uncle, and the feeling was mutual. By the time Roderick left the state capital, he'd secured a job and bought a comfortable house for him and Betsy to live in.

The distance from Sacramento back to Virginia City was only a fraction of his original trip from New York City, but it somehow seemed longer. He couldn't wait to see Betsy again and to hold her close. He missed her terribly, which he supposed was normal for people in love, but his impatience also stemmed from something else. Worry. For no good reason, he worried that leaving Betsy even for that short time had been a mistake. Relief would only come from seeing her again.

Two days before he'd set out for his return journey, he'd sent Betsy a telegram, informing her about the good news of his new job and letting her know the date and time of his arrival in Virginia City. He'd expected to receive a reply from her, but when he checked at the telegraph office before boarding the train, no reply waited for him. Logically, he knew this wasn't anything to be alarmed about. There could be many benign reasons why she'd been unable to reply or the message didn't make it to him in time. Still, the lack of communication from her only added to his needling fear that something was wrong and made him even more impatient to be back with her in Virginia City.

After what seemed like ages, but in actuality was only a few days, the train reached its stop in Virginia City. Roderick peered out the window, looking for Betsy, but she wasn't on the platform. He tried to settle his wild thoughts, but his anxiety reached an all-time high. He hastened to his room at the hotel. Not bothering to freshen up, he dropped his suitcase there and headed immediately for Betsy's cabin at a jog.

When he reached his destination, he stood outside momentarily, trying to catch his breath. Before he fully succeeded at that, he knocked on the door. He could hear some murmuring and movement inside before the door opened and Lou appeared in the doorway. The worried, sad frown on her face nearly knocked Roderick over.

"Mrs. Blake? Is everything all right?" he asked.

She shook her head and looked down. "I'm afraid not, Roderick."

"What's wrong?" he asked, trying to keep the panic out of his voice.

Lou nibbled at her bottom lip. "I don't know how to explain it, but… something is different about Betsy. We don't understand it. It happened shortly after you left, and her pa and I can't figure out the cause."

Roderick had to talk himself out of tearing past Lou into the house. "What? Is she ill? Is she hurt?"

Lou shook her head quickly and reached out to touch his arm. "No, it's nothing like that. She is perfectly well. It's just…"

"What?" Roderick asked, hearing the desperation in his voice. "What in God's name is going on?"

"She doesn't want to see you." Lou's words tumbled out quickly.

The revelation hit him like a punch in the stomach, knocking out all the air from his lungs. When he found his voice, he said, "I don't understand."

"Neither do we," Lou responded.

Timothy appeared next to his wife in the doorway. Neither made an offer to allow Roderick entrance. They seemed wary of him, Timothy even more so than Lou. "She won't tell us why," Timothy said. "Only that she no longer wishes to marry you. She asked me to give you this." He opened his palm, which contained the diamond engagement ring.

Roderick barely glanced at it. "I won't accept that ring back, and I won't accept the end of this courtship without hearing why from her," he said, his voice rising in volume. "I insist on speaking with her."

Lou and Timothy exchanged glances.

"Betsy!" Roderick called past them. He couldn't even begin to guess why this was happening. All he knew was that he felt like his entire world was upside down and didn't make sense. He needed to see his girl.

Betsy came into his view, which gave him a measure of relief until he saw her face. Roderick frowned with concern. She looked in his direction, but it was as though she was looking through him, not at him. "It's all right," she told her parents. "I'll talk to him." Her pa gave her shoulder a squeeze before he and Lou moved so that Betsy could join Roderick outside. A moment later the door was closed and Betsy and Roderick were alone.

It was all Roderick could do not to take her into his arms and hold her tight, but her demeanor was such that she didn't welcome his presence, let alone his embrace. "Tell me what happened, Betsy. I'm so confused."

Betsy set her jaw and stared at him, her eyes cold. When she spoke, it was without emotion. "I've decided I do not wish to marry you, Roderick."

Even though he'd been told this already by Timothy, hearing the words from Betsy caused a new wave of shock and pain. "But why? What changed your mind? I love you more than anything, and I know you love me too!"

"I don't love you, Roderick," she said evenly. "I thought I did, but while you were gone I realized we are not meant to be together. I'm better suited for a man from around here. Please forgive me for leading you on for so long."

"Hogwash!" Roderick exclaimed. "That makes absolutely no sense. Only a few short weeks ago you stood on the train platform with tears in your eyes, grateful to me for seeing about this job nearby so that we could be together. You accepted my proposal. We... we were intimate. And now I'm supposed to believe you don't love me? Something must have happened, and I must know what it was."

"Nothing happened," she insisted coldly. "Remember before you left for Sacramento, you told me that anything I wished for, you would grant. I'm asking you now to move back to New York and forget about me. That is my only wish now."

Roderick studied her eyes, glancing back and forth between each cold depth, searching to find a reason for her words. He looked for some crack in her expression, some sign that she still cared about him. He studied her lips for trembling, the same lips that had previously kissed him so passionately. Was all of their love a lie?

No, their love was not a lie. He was sure of it. What she was doing now, whatever the cause, that had to be the lie. Clearing his throat, he said softly, "If it's truly your wish for me to leave you and return to New York, then I will. But I'm not yet convinced that's what you want, and I aim to find out what took place while I was gone." His voice cracked with emotion.

When his voice wavered, he witnessed a flash of sorrow and compassion in Betsy's gaze. It was subtle, and it happened so fast that if Roderick hadn't been staring into her eyes at that exact moment, he would have missed it entirely. *That* was what he'd been trying to find, and it gave him hope. She cared that he was in pain.

Cowboy up, he told himself. Figure out what's going on.

Straightening, he scrubbed a hand around his face. He was in need of a bath, a shave, and a good night's sleep. "I'll be on my way, Betsy. Good night." He gave her a quick bow and turned to walk back to town. He half-expected her to stop him, but she said nothing. When he glanced over his shoulder after he'd walked a minute or so, she wasn't there. His heart constricted painfully. Not only did she not try to stop him from leaving, she hadn't watched his retreat. All signs pointed to being serious about no longer wanting to be with him. It was only that brief flash of compassion in her eyes that gave him hope. That was what he would cling to until he solved the mystery of her change of heart.

***

The next evening, Roderick set out for the Harringtons' cabin. If Betsy and her parents couldn't give him answers, his next best bet was Adam and Susannah. He brought with him a bottle of Beam whiskey, which he knew was Adam's favorite.

He arrived around eight o'clock, which was near the children's bedtime. Susannah answered the door. "Hello, Roderick," she said, not sounding surprised at seeing him. "Please come in." Her voice was sad, which told him that she knew about Betsy's decision, but she was warm toward him. He appreciated that she didn't treat him as the enemy, which was the feeling he'd gotten from Timothy. It was natural for Betsy's father to be wary of him after his daughter's strange change of heart, but his coldness had stung Roderick regardless.

"Forgive me for calling on you so late," Roderick said. "I'm hoping to get some answers about Betsy, and I thought it would be best to discuss the matter with you and Mr. Harrington after the children were in bed." He handed her the whiskey.

"There's no need to apologize. You're welcome here anytime. Come with me and I'll pour the three of us some of this. Then we can talk in the sitting room." She led the way to the kitchen.

Caleb and Mini were still awake, sitting at the small table and drinking warm milk. After they greeted Roderick politely at Susannah's prompting, she said, "You two get yourselves to bed after you're done with the milk. Your pa and I need to talk to Mr. Mason. Caleb, help Mini with washing her face. Mini, don't give your brother any trouble."

"I'll be good, Mama!" she said cheerfully.

Handing Roderick his glass of whiskey, Susannah motioned for him to follow her to the sitting room. Adam was sitting in his armchair reading a paper from New York. When he saw Roderick, he set it aside and stood. "Roderick, good to see you." He held out his hand. Like his wife's demeanor, his was sympathetic and welcoming.

Roderick sat on the sofa and drew a deep breath. Susannah handed Adam his whiskey before sitting in her rocking chair close to the fire with her own glass. She stared into the flames licking over the wood and sipped her drink, appearing a bit removed from the men to allow them to speak with her there as a silent listener.

"I appreciate you two taking the time to talk to me and for being so welcoming," Roderick said. The sadness he felt was suffocating, but he knew it would be even worse if he had no friends. He fished into his pocket for his pipe. "Do you mind?" he asked Susannah.

She shook her head. "No, please make yourself comfortable."

Roderick nodded his thanks. He struck a match and lit the tobacco.

Adam drank some of the whiskey from his glass and then twirled the liquid around. "I'm sure you want answers about Betsy's decision, but I'm afraid we won't be of much use to you. Believe me when I say Susannah and I have tried to figure out her reasoning, but we can't understand it at all."

"It makes no sense," Roderick said, shaking his head. "When I stood on the train's platform and said goodbye to her, I'd never been surer of anything than I was of Betsy's love. I don't know what could have happened in a few short weeks to change it."

"It's a mystery, all right," Adam said, leaning back. "Mostly I heard about this situation from Timothy, but I did ask her directly about it yesterday."

Roderick was impatient to know every word that passed between Adam and Betsy. At that moment, however, Mini burst into the room, followed by Caleb, who appeared to be trying to stop her. She headed straight for Roderick and sat down next to him on the sofa, obviously excited about having company and unwilling to miss out on anything by sleeping.

"Mini, I told you to go to bed," Susannah said sharply. She frowned at Caleb, who held up his hands.

"I tried to stop her, Ma, but she ran out here quick as a fox."

"Go to bed, kids," Adam said mildly, and returned his attention to Roderick. "When I asked Betsy what happened, the only thing she said was that it would be better for everyone if you left."

That explanation only baffled him further. "Better for everyone how? What could that possibly mean? It's like she's a different person! Before I left, she was one way, and now she has completely changed."

Caleb piped up. "Yeah, she went batty after that man came here and talked to her."

The room went silent. All three adults turned and stared at the boy for a moment before Adam cleared his throat and spoke. "Who, son? What man?"

The boy shrugged. "I don't know his name. But when Betsy was here with me and Mini while you and Ma were in town, I saw a man talking to her over by the barn. When the man left and she came inside, she didn't hardly speak for the rest of the time. Just stared at the wall. Wouldn't even answer my questions about homework."

Adam's eyebrows headed north. He turned and looked at Roderick, who was experiencing a strange mixture of hope and rage. Swallowing it down, he addressed Caleb. "Did you see what the man looked like, son?"

Caleb looked up, accessing his memory, before saying, "He was tall and he had hair like mine. Light in color."

Roderick's hands clenched into fists. The man described could be a number of people, but it almost certainly was Johnny. "I thought we took care of that problem," Roderick growled.

Adam nodded solemnly. "I thought we did too."

"I'll kill the bastard," Roderick spat, and then felt badly at having cursed. "Forgive me, I forgot myself in front of the children," he said to Susannah, who only smiled at him with understanding.

Adam set his glass of whiskey on the table with a thud. "Mini shouldn't be here to begin with." He frowned at his daughter. "Get yourself to bed, young lady. Right now."

"But Pa, I'm thirsty," Mini whined.

Roderick had to admire the little girl. If he'd heard Adam's barked command as a child, he imagined he would have rushed to obey. Mini seemed in no hurry to do so.

Adam's eyebrows drew together. "I'm not going to say it again, Mini, and if I have to get up and take you to bed instead of you getting there on your own two legs, you're going to be in a heap of trouble. Understand?"

That warning seemed to be motivation enough for her to obey, though not quickly by any means. She slid down from the sofa slower than molasses on a February morning and flashed Adam a put-upon frown as though he'd asked her to do something very unfair.

His expression remained stern. He crooked his finger at her, indicating she was to go to him, and she obeyed, dragging her feet. She seemed to know she was in for a talking-to because she stared down when she reached him.

"When your ma tells you to go to bed, what are you supposed to do?" he scolded.

"Go to bed," she said in a small voice.

"And when I tell you to go to bed, what are you supposed to do?"

She hesitated for a moment. "Give you a hug and kiss and then go to bed."

In spite of the serious mood in the room, Roderick had to stifle a laugh. The youngest Harrington was a tiny little thing, but she was smart as a whip. She knew just what to say to soften Adam's heart and get herself out of trouble. Susannah snickered in the background.

Adam groaned. He tilted his head back and looked to the heavens. "God help me, I don't think I'll survive this child." He shook his head and pulled Mini into his arms for a quick hug, gave her a kiss on the top of her head, and turned her in the direction of the door. "Get to bed, little lady, and get a wiggle on. I'd better not see you 'til the sun comes up." He gave her bottom a smack to send her on her way. A moment later, Mini disappeared out the door.

Adam ran a hand over his face. "I've always been too lenient with her, and I admit after the hornet scare I'm spoiling her more."

"We all are," Susannah said. "Even Caleb has put himself at that child's beck and call."

The boy nodded. "I never want to see her cry again. It was just awful." He turned to leave, but Adam stopped him.

"Son, come sit down, please."

Caleb walked to the sofa where Mini had been sitting previously and took a seat. Roderick addressed him.

"So you say Betsy acted strangely after seeing this man, son?"

"Yeah, it was like she was scared, but not in the normal way, like when you come across a rattler. She didn't run or scream. She just sat at the table and stared at the wall."

"Sounds like she was in shock," Adam said, shaking his head.

Susannah drank the last sip of her whiskey. "Poor Betsy. Johnny must have put the fear of God into her somehow."

Roderick bit back another oath. He recalled the strange look of fear that had appeared on Betsy's face the night of the barn dance, and he reckoned that was the expression Caleb referred to.

"I wonder what he said to her," Susannah mused.

"There's no use speculating," Adam said. "We'll ask her to come to supper tomorrow and get to the bottom of it."

Roderick took a long drag from his pipe, thinking about how the conversation between Betsy and the rest of them might go. "Sounds like a good idea, but I suppose you shouldn't mention that I'll be here when you invite her. She said she doesn't want to see me again." Saying the words pained him, but there was no avoiding the truth of what he'd been told.

Adam nodded at Caleb. "You can get to bed now. Thank you for telling us about this, son, and I also want to thank you for being such a good brother to Mini. You're turning into a man before my very eyes."

Caleb beamed as he stood, clearly pleased about his father's praise.

"Yes, I'm grateful to you too," Roderick seconded. "Now we have some idea about how to proceed with Betsy."

"It wasn't anything, Mr. Mason," Caleb said with a shy shrug. He walked to Adam. "Since I'm so grown up, can I have some whiskey, Pa?"

Adam raised a brow. After a moment's consideration, he picked up his glass from the table and handed it to him. "One sip."

Caleb drank the liquor and made a face as soon as he swallowed it, which made Adam chuckle as he took back the glass. "It's an acquired taste. One I hope you don't acquire for some time yet."

He shook his head. "Don't think I ever will."

"That's just fine if you don't," he said with a wink.

Caleb said goodnight to everyone and left the room. Roderick took a final puff from his pipe and stood to leave as well. "I've taken up enough of your time. Sure do appreciate you all."

Adam and Susannah stood to walk him to the door. "We're your friends, Roderick, no matter what happens," Susannah said.

Chapter Twelve

Betsy stumbled through the activities of the day, feeling as though she was wading upstream in a high-current river. Everything was a chore that brought her no pleasure. Before she saw Roderick, she'd been sad about what she had to do. After seeing him and witnessing the hurt on his face, she felt so devastated she could hardly breathe.

She'd known it would be hard to reject him, despite it being the right thing to do. She did not know, however, just how truly difficult it would be. Upon seeing him standing in front of her cabin, disheveled and heartbroken, it had taken everything in her power not to wrap her arms around him. The look in his eye was close to panic, but there was nothing she could do to alleviate his pain or hers. People's lives depended on Roderick returning to New York.

Susannah stopped by while Betsy fed the horses, slowly tossing hay into their stalls at a pace half her usual speed. Her older friend walked straight up to her and wrapped her arms around her in a tight hug. "Hello, sweetheart."

Her greeting was so kind that Betsy nearly burst into tears. She swallowed and returned the hug. Susannah, like everyone else, didn't know the great secret Betsy kept, but her compassion felt like a temporary salve to her wounds.

Releasing her, Susannah said, "You're coming to supper at our house tonight. I'm baking a new kind of bread, raisin cinnamon, and I want your honest opinion on it."

It was an order, not an invitation, but it didn't matter one way or the other to Betsy. Whether she ate with the Harringtons or ate with her parents, it was all the same to her. "Sure, Mrs. Harrington. Thank you." Her voice sounded weary to her own ears, and she hoped Susannah wouldn't think her rude. She didn't have the will to muster up any enthusiasm.

Her friend didn't seem offended. "Excellent!" she responded cheerfully. "Come by about six-o'clock. I'll see you then."

For the next few hours, Betsy continued her chores. She frequently swiped at a tear that would escape, but after some time she felt too sad and tired even to cry. She'd never known a loss such as this, and she didn't know how to find relief. She knew plenty of people who cared about her, but since no one could know what troubled her, no one could effectively comfort her.

Betsy obediently trudged to the Harringtons' at six-o'clock. She'd changed into a clean dress, but she hadn't brushed her hair or washed her face after the day's labor.

She knew she appeared a fright, but she couldn't find it in herself to care.

The scent of the baking bread reached her before she reached the Harringtons' cabin. Her mouth watered of its own accord and she realized she hadn't eaten anything that day besides half a bowl of porridge in the morning. Betsy walked around to the back of the cabin to enter through the kitchen as she normally did. Susannah was next to the counter, slicing freshly baked bread. She paused in her chore to usher Betsy to a chair and to place in front of her three slices of bread slathered with butter. Despite Betsy's general lack of appetite, the wonderful scent of cinnamon and raisins was enough to compel her to eat. She made quick work of the snack.

"What do you think of my new recipe?"

Betsy swallowed her last bite. "It's delicious," she said, and meant it. "I haven't been feeling like eating lately, but that was so good I had to eat every last bite."

Susannah smiled appreciatively, and Betsy noticed, as she often did, how beautiful Susannah was. Even after laboring over a hot stove, she looked like a sophisticated lady, everything Betsy aspired to be and wasn't. Sadness hit her then, thinking about how Roderick had made her feel beautiful and sophisticated. She'd never find another man who looked at her with the same adoration. Tears sprang to her eyes but, before she could sink further into sadness, Susannah wiped her floured hands on her apron and said, "Let's go to the dining area, shall we?" She untied the ribbon of her apron and tossed it on the counter. "I've fed the kids and put the roast and fixins' on the table, so supper is ready, just with us adults."

Betsy nodded and stood from where she sat at the small table. Though she didn't say so, she was relieved that the children wouldn't be in attendance. Every time she saw them, she thought about what Johnny had said. She shook her head, trying to free her tortured mind from the memory.

With her face downcast, Betsy followed Susannah through the door to the dining room. She heard the scraping of chairs and looked up to find Adam and Roderick standing to greet her. She froze, and her gaze flitted wildly to Susannah, feeling betrayed at what she realized was a setup to bring her and Roderick together. She was glad she wasn't holding anything, for she surely would have dropped it in that moment. Her eyes flooded with tears and the whole room became blurry. She was only dimly aware of Susannah's arm circling her shoulders.

Before when she'd faced Roderick, she'd been prepared and had practiced maintaining a cold, composed countenance. Now that she'd been caught off-guard, her emotions skittered around like a horse with no reins. Roderick was looking at her with love and worry. She couldn't bear it for another moment. She heard Susannah's voice. "We're going to help you, Betsy. We know Johnny scared you."

Terror shot down Betsy's spine. They weren't supposed to know that! She shook herself out of Susannah's grasp and backed away toward the door. "Please," she begged, looking at Roderick through tear-filled eyes. "Please forget about me and leave Virginia City. It's not safe here!"

"Betsy, come sit down and explain to us why it's not safe," Roderick said, his voice kind but firm.

She shook her head violently. "I can't!" She turned and opened the door. She needed to get away. She couldn't risk Johnny seeing her there with Roderick, so she fled in the direction of her cabin.

Immediately she became aware of Roderick's heavy footsteps falling behind her. "No!" she screamed.

The ground was flat and barren, and it took no time at all for him to catch up with her. Without speaking, he swooped her up over his shoulder, clamped one arm around the back of her knees, and strode back to the Harringtons' house.

Frantic and enraged, Betsy pounded on his back with her fists. "Let me go, Roderick! You don't understand."

He didn't speak to her until he'd carried her into the Harringtons' cabin and set her down on a chair next to the table. Placing a hand on both shoulders to prevent her from standing, he said, "You're right, darling, I don't understand. You're going to explain it to me. To us," he added, glancing at Adam and Susannah. "Every person in this room loves you and wants to help you, and you don't need to deal with whatever scared you alone."

Tears streamed down her face. She shook her head. "You think I don't want to tell you? I do, more than anything. But it would be selfish of me, just so I feel better. I won't sacrifice everyone's safety just so I don't feel so alone!"

Roderick sat on a chair next to her and wrapped an arm around her shoulders. He pulled her to his chest, and she couldn't find the will to fight him. "Darling, it's not your job to protect everyone."

"He's right," Adam said, his voice lacking Roderick's patience. "Protecting people is my job, your father's, and Roderick's. Now you look here, Betsy. I've had just about enough of your nonsense. You tell us what happened while we were away and you were here watching the kids. Caleb saw you talking to Johnny, and I demand to know what he said to you."

Betsy jerked away from Roderick and jumped to her feet. "Caleb saw it? Oh, God. Where is he? Is he all right?"

"He's in his room, and he's just fine. Sit your ass down," Adam barked, pointing at the chair.

Betsy sank back onto the chair immediately, a reflexive action after receiving the sharp order, and Susannah handed her a glass of milk. Glaring at her husband, she said, "You might be a little patient with Betsy. She needs our understanding and support, not you bellowing at her."

"She'll get my understanding and support," Adam shot back, "just as soon as she tells us what this is about."

Betsy drank the entire glass of milk, mostly to give her an excuse not to talk during that time, and thought about what she should say. She looked at Roderick, who was observing her with pain in his eyes but also determination. She realized they wouldn't allow her to leave the cabin that evening before telling them what happened. Though that thought frightened her terribly, she felt a measure of relief. They weren't giving her any choice in the matter, so she didn't have to make any more painful decisions; she only had to obey.

She'd apparently used up Roderick's supply of patience in addition to Adam's. He leaned over and said softly in her ear so that only she could hear, "Are you going to start talking, or do I need to take you to the barn and strap you first?"

Ironically, the threat actually helped to alleviate more of her fear. Recalling his strength allowed her to hope his strength was enough to solve this problem. "All right," Betsy moaned. She set the empty glass on the table and folded her hands in her lap. Staring down at them, she relayed the details of her confrontation with Johnny.

Johnny had said that he wasn't going to lose her to Roderick and that if she didn't convince him to return to where he came from, everyone would pay. Johnny had gone into great detail about how they each would pay, so Betsy provided them with the same details, starting with Roderick.

It turned out that Johnny had not only been stalking Betsy, but had actually stalked everyone close to her. He knew Roderick's exact routine and had somehow been able to discover it without once being seen. By the time Betsy got around to telling the room Johnny's threats again Caleb and Mini, she was shaking. He had detailed everything about the children, from where they did their chores to where Caleb's fishing hole was to what time they went to bed.

What had terrified her most of all was Johnny's description about how exactly he would hurt the children, at which point Adam stopped her. "I think we've heard enough, Betsy," he said, his voice much gentler than before. He reached over and took Susannah's hand in his and squeezed it.

Betsy looked at Roderick, blinking away tears. "I-I didn't feel I had a choice when I rejected you so terribly. I had to protect you even though it broke my heart."

Roderick's gaze was kind and forgiving. "I understand, darling. Come here." He patted his leg to indicate he wanted her to sit in his lap.

Though Betsy might normally have felt embarrassed at doing so in front of other people, at that moment she wanted nothing more than for him to hold her. She sat on his lap and curled up against him, still crying as he held her. He murmured comforting words against her hair and stroked her back.

"It's all my fault," she cried. "If anything happens it'll be all my fault."

"No, that's not true," Roderick said. "No one is to blame for this but Johnny, and we're going to take care of him, don't worry."

Betsy pulled away so she could look at him. "That's what you said before. But after you all visited him, he only seemed to get angrier and scarier."

Roderick brought her back into the hug. "We'll put our heads together and come up with a new way to fix this, once and for all. One man doesn't get to choose whether you and I can be together."

Susannah stood. The blood had drained from her face, and her voice wavered when she spoke. "I'm going to check on the children and then get Mini to bed."

"Bring them out for a minute so I can tell them good night, would you, darlin'?" Adam's voice was strained. Though he didn't appear frightened like his wife, anxiety could be heard in his voice.

Susannah nodded and left the room. A short time later she returned with Caleb and Mini, who went to where Adam sat.

"I'm going to bed and I'm not arguing," Mini informed her father proudly.

Adam didn't smile. He held her face in his hands for a moment, studying her. "You're my good girl." He kissed her forehead. "Good night, sweetheart." Mini gave him a hug before rejoining her ma near the door.

"'Night, Pa," Caleb said, and gave him a kiss on his cheek.

Adam grabbed him into a bear hug. When he released him, he said, "Son, I need you to help me all day tomorrow at the range."

A look of surprise crossed Caleb's face. "But I have school tomorrow."

"Yes, I know, and I'm sorry about that. But a few things have come up and I could use your help."

"Sure," Caleb said, sounding confused.

"Get some sleep. I'll explain more tomorrow."

After Caleb and Mini left the room, Adam said to Susannah, "Until this matter with Johnny is resolved, I don't want Caleb to go off to school alone. As far as you and Mini are concerned, I want you here at home with the doors locked."

Roderick gave Betsy a squeeze. "I don't want you anywhere alone either."

Betsy shook her head. "Same goes for you, Roderick. We're all in danger."

147

"We'll go to the marshal tomorrow and insist he do something this time," Roderick said.

"That won't work," Betsy moaned. "The marshal won't help us!"

"She's right, he won't," Adam said grimly. "We'll have to take matters into our own hands again."

"What else can you do besides lambaste him?" Susannah asked. "Like Betsy said, it didn't work last time, and neither did the report to the marshal. Something different must be done."

"Let's think about that," Roderick said. "What do we know about this man, other than the fact he's obsessed with Betsy?"

Adam shrugged. "He's a cowboy. Worked for me a month or so before I fired him. He's lazy and clearly disturbed."

"What does he care about? What's important to him?" Roderick asked.

"Money," Betsy responded. "Doesn't have any family about, but he cares about lining his pockets. He was enraged about losing his job on account of me."

Roderick rubbed his chin. "I suppose I could pay him off. Tell him that in exchange for money, he has to leave town."

"No fucking way," Adam said, and slammed his fist on the table. "You are *not* going to reward that bastard."

"I don't like the idea either," Roderick said tersely, "but if it works, I'm willing to go down that route."

"How about we do the opposite?" Susannah suggested. "Adam, you're good friends with Mr. Taylor, the banker. Ask him to drain his account, leave him with nothing. Hit him where it hurts."

"That's illegal. Taylor would never agree to it," Adam grunted.

The four of them fell silent and stared at each other, stumped. The only suggestion presented thus far that could work was Roderick's, but none of them liked his idea. It offended their sense of justice.

After some time, Susannah spoke quietly in a conspiratorial voice. "I know what we can do."

Everyone perked up and looked at her. Her tone indicated an idea worth listening to. After she explained it, they knew they had found their answer.

Chapter Thirteen

Betsy's and Roderick's wedding was a simple affair. Only Betsy's family and the Harringtons were in attendance. Originally they planned to make a grand event of it and invite most of the townsfolk, but Betsy preferred not to spend time planning and instead to be married right away so that she could move in with Roderick at the hotel. He preferred this as well, since he could better protect her if she lived with him.

They arranged to move to California in three weeks' time. The two of them were excited to start their life together in their new home, but they wanted to stay in Virginia City long enough to see justice being served to Johnny and to ensure that none of his dire threats came to fruition. Susannah and Adam kept close watch over their children, never letting them out of their sight, and the Blakes hired a man from town to guard the house while they slept.

Betsy apologized multiple times to Roderick for responding as she did to Johnny's threats. "I'll never forget the look on your face when I told you I didn't love you," she said to him tearfully one evening. "I'll never forgive myself for causing you that pain."

Roderick set aside the paper he was reading and directed a stern look at the beautiful woman who was now his wife. He'd told her time and time again she was not the one to blame. Her actions had come from a place of love, as far as he was concerned, and he blamed Johnny entirely for the pain he had felt.

"You were traumatized, darling. What do I need to do so you forgive yourself?"

She threw her hands in the air. "I don't know! Punish me, maybe."

"Very well," he said, straightening in his seat. He placed a hand over each knee. "Come here and I'll punish you. Then I never want to hear another word about how terrible you feel."

She must not have expected him to agree to her suggestion so quickly. Her eyes widened and she hedged. "Well, maybe I don't need a punishment. It was just one suggestion. Weren't we going to come up with more?"

Roderick laughed. "No, I think punishment is just what you need." He crooked his finger, indicating she was to come to him.

She stared at him with a concerned look into her eyes, making no move to obey, which caused Roderick's brow to slowly lift. "Are you going to make me catch you, Betsy? You know that will only add to the punishment."

She sighed. "You have to promise not to spank me too hard before I go to you."

He snorted a laugh. "I don't believe you have any say over that. Besides, who said anything about spanking? There are other punishments."

The worried expression on her face morphed into curiosity. "Like what?"

He did not respond, instead giving her a hard look that indicated he wasn't going to debate or discuss it further. She sighed again and walked to him.

"Take off all your clothes," he said, leaning back and crossing his arms.

A glint of lust and excitement lit her eyes, and she obeyed immediately. He felt his cock straining against his trousers as she revealed every inch of her beautiful body to him. When she was fully naked, he said, "Place your hands on the back of your head and turn around."

She bit her lip and obeyed. He stood and planted kisses along the nape of her neck and bare shoulders before he ran his hand down her back and over the slope of her bottom. He gave her cheek a crisp spank, causing her to jump and emit a yelp.

"Go bend over the bed," he ordered.

She did as directed but said in a saucy voice, "I thought you weren't going to spank me."

He grunted. "I didn't say that, and don't be smart. Reach behind you, take hold of your bottom cheeks, and spread them apart for me."

She gasped and looked at him over her shoulder. Since she did not immediately do as he asked, he strode to the bed and landed six very hard swats on her bottom, causing her to yelp loudly.

"Do as I say, don't argue, and don't delay," he said firmly. "This is punishment, and I won't tolerate a moment of disobedience."

She groaned, but she obediently reached back and parted her now-pink bottom cheeks, revealing to his view her bottom hole and entrance to her womanhood.

"I'm going downstairs and you're going to stay just like that until I return. Do you understand?"

She whimpered, and he could see the embarrassment heating her face. "Where are you going, Roderick?"

"Was that an answer to my question?" he asked, raising his voice.

"No," she moaned, and buried her face in the quilt.

Roderick slipped off the thin belt from around his waist and wound it around his hand until only a short strip was free. "When you don't answer my questions during discipline, you will be punished further," he informed her. "Now you stay in position for this, keep your cheeks spread." He first gently tapped the strap between the split of her cheeks. Then he whipped her sensitive little bottom hole four times.

"Oh, god, Roderick!" she screamed, keeping her bottom cheeks spread but jerking her head back and forth, trying to absorb the sting.

He tossed the belt aside. "Let's try it again. I'm going downstairs and you're going to stay just like that until I return. Do you understand?"

"Yes!" she cried. "God, yes!"

He reached out to touch her sex, discovering that she was already slick with desire from the humiliation. "Dirty little girl likes getting her bottom hole spanked, huh?" He landed a swat on her pussy. She moaned, and her face flushed even redder. "That's what I thought," he said, and wiped her juices off his hand onto her back.

He left the room and headed downstairs. As he strode outside toward a plant he'd noticed for weeks, the image of her naked and bent over the bed with her cheeks spread remained in his mind. His cock was engorged, tightening his trousers uncomfortably. He looked forward to burying his manhood deep inside of her later.

But first things first. He reached down and pulled up the plant, exposing the thick, bulbous gingerroot. Yes, that would serve his purposes perfectly. He trimmed off the stems and leaves, leaving only the root, and walked back to the room.

"Good girl," he said, when he entered to find her obediently in the same position. He dunked the root in the basin of water in their room and cleaned off the dirt. He then sat down on a chair across the room, where he could do some whittling while staring at his wife in such a wonderfully exposed position.

As he skinned and shaped the ginger, he prepared her for what was coming. "I've got a very special punishment in mind for my very special girl," he explained. "In my hand is gingerroot. God created it to punish naughty girls' bottoms."

"He did not!" she protested. "It's to flavor food."

He bit back a laugh and continued. "I'm going to place it up your bottom hole, and you're going to feel a great deal of burning for about ten minutes. Then it will slowly fade away."

She moaned, and her response came out in thick, aroused voice. "That sounds painful."

"It is. It's a punishment that's been used for a very long time on naughty females. It was first used on disobedient slaves on the other side of the world. Their masters would bend them over a bench and restrain their hands and legs so that they couldn't move at all. Then they would slip the instrument of punishment into their bottoms and watch them writhe, listening to their moans of pain. You've been moaning for weeks about not forgiving yourself. After this, I think you'll feel properly punished and able to."

"All right, Roderick," she said breathlessly.

He could hear the submission and trust in her voice, which pleased him greatly. "If the slaves were especially bad, they would get their bottoms whipped while the gingerroot plugged them."

She whimpered at the thought. "That was very mean of their masters."

"Mm hmm," Roderick agreed. He held out the root in front of him, admiring its shape and size, and then stood and walked to Betsy.

He pressed the tip of the bulb against her rosette, twisting it slightly. "Relax and open for me, take your punishment," he said sternly.

"I'm trying," she whimpered, her pucker contracting nervously. He pressed the ginger forward, gently but insistently, and gradually her bottom opened and accepted the intrusion.

"You may release your bottom cheeks now, darling."

She obeyed and folded her arms under her chin. "That feels cold, not hot," she told him, wriggling her bottom in the air a little.

"It's going to heat up gradually and you'll soon feel a nearly unbearable burn. It won't harm you, though. It only hurts in the moment. And you should be grateful I am a kind master. In the past, if a slave had done something especially bad or was not silent during the punishment, her master would remove the gingerroot after the effect wore off, peel off another layer, and place it in her bottom again. And again and again for as long as it took for her to learn their lesson."

"Ohh," she said, and then the pitch of her voice became higher. "Oh my god!"

"I see it's starting to work." Roderick reached out and pinched her bottom cheeks together, bringing her bottom hole in close contact with the ginger for maximum burn.

"OWWW!" she screeched. She reached back frantically to grasp the offending implement to yank it out.

"No, that's a bad girl," Roderick said. He captured both of her wrists in one hand and pinned them against her lower back, while continuing to pinch her bottom cheeks together. Her only free body parts were her legs, which she kicked frantically. "Please, Roderick, take it out! I forgive myself!" She twisted, but to no avail, for he kept her firmly in place.

"Relax and accept your discipline," he said implacably. "While you are experiencing this burning, think about the pain you and I felt when someone came close to destroying our relationship. Imagine this is the last of

156

it, and when it goes away, it's gone for good. Nothing will come between us again."

She continued thrashing around for a few more seconds, and then something seemed to break inside of her as his words sunk in. She settled on the bed and burst into tears. Roderick could tell his words had hit just the right spot and that her cries were cleansing. He continued to hold her wrists in one hand but released his pinch so that he could stroke her bottom and thighs. "Good girl. Accept the pain and cry all you need to, darling."

She nodded and sobbed during the rest of the discipline. Roderick could see that as the pain from the ginger subsided, so too did the pain from her action. Minutes ticked by slowly, until finally her cries died down. She let out a sigh of contentment. "It doesn't burn as much anymore."

Roderick released her wrists and removed the ginger plug from her bottom. "I've got to have you now," he said, hearing the thick arousal in his voice. "You have no idea how aroused that made me, punishing your cute little bottom hole." He undid the button of his trousers and dropped them to the floor, causing his erection to spring forward.

Betsy turned around, reached out and unbuttoned his shirt. "I want you too," she said breathily.

Roderick tore the shirt off his shoulders after Betsy finished unbuttoning. He placed his hands on the backs of her soft, firm thighs and pushed her toward the center of the bed, where he climbed over her, straddling her hips.

She tilted her pelvis forward, inviting his invasion into her core, and Roderick didn't need a second invitation. He placed the head of his cock along her slick entrance and then buried himself fully inside her snug channel. Relishing the feeling for a moment, he leaned forward and captured her lips with his. He then began his movements, first slowly, a strong caress. He nibbled on her neck and growled in her ear. "Is your naughty bottom still a little warm?"

"Yes!" she gasped, tilting her head back and giving him access to the center of her delicate neck. He wrapped his hand around her throat and applied slight pressure, pinning her on the bed. His cock claimed her body, becoming more insistent in its demand for pleasure from her as his pace quickened.

Betsy dragged her nails down his chest before clutching his muscled arms and hanging on for the ride. His thrusts were hard and fast, driving her breasts up and down until he released her neck, took one of them in his hand and slapped the other lightly. She squealed from the sudden swat to her erect nipple and moaned when he bent down and caught it in between his lips before grazing it with his teeth.

He disconnected from her briefly in order to turn her around and take her pussy from behind. Slowing his movements, he slapped her bottom hard as it bounced against his stomach. He slid his hand up her back, up her neck and finally around to her mouth. His fingers invaded her hot mouth. "Suck me," he ordered in a low growl. She obeyed, obediently lapping at him and wetting his thumb sloppily with her saliva. His digit now properly lubricated, he touched her punished bottom hole.

"*Unngghhhh,*" she cried unintelligibly as he pressed his thumb into her rosette until it was fully buried. Her cheeks flushed scarlet. "Roderick…" she gasped.

He sped up his movements, fucking her hard while keeping her hot bottom filled with his thumb, and it wasn't long before she arched her back and screamed out her orgasm. Her sex clenched around him, milking his cock and causing his pleasure to build rapidly.

"I'm going to come, baby," he groaned, right before he stiffened and erupted inside of her. He collapsed on top of her, using his arms to partially prop himself so that he didn't land all of his weight on her. When he'd caught his breath, he kissed her temple. What a treasure she was, accepting his discipline and finding pleasure with him afterwards.

Later, after they'd bathed and were still swimming in the afterglow of lovemaking, Roderick lay on his back in the bed and brought Betsy to his chest. "How are you feeling, little lamb?"

She sighed, a contented look on her face. "I feel happy and loved."

"Not guilty any longer?"

"No." She wrapped her arm around him and snuggled against him.

"I love you being here like this in my arms, allowing me to hold and possess you."

"You'll always possess me. I'll always be yours," she told him.

He kissed her forehead. "I've lost count of the times I've had to chase and catch you, and I don't see it stopping anytime soon. But you're right, darling, even if you run a thousand more times, I'll always catch you and get you back into my arms where you belong. The wolf always catches the lamb."

"Thank you, Roderick, but I won't run again," she whispered, her eyes half lidded.

"Yes, you will." He stroked her hair and held her as she drifted off to sleep.

He smiled to himself, thinking about their time together. He had traveled across the country to catch her, and it had been the best decision of his life. He knew that, whatever their future held, whatever came their way, he'd always make the same decision. He'd forever and always be up to the task of catching Betsy.

Epilogue

On May 23, 1899, the marshal marched Johnny Miller to the jail in handcuffs. His crime: Bank robbery. His sentence: 23 years in federal prison.

The brilliant idea of how to rid themselves of Johnny came from Susannah, and further discussion and planning allowed the four of them to concoct the perfect setup. With Mr. Taylor's knowledge and the marshal's oversight, they used Johnny's penchant for making an easy buck to their advantage. Susannah and Adam had a conversation within Johnny's range of hearing that went something like this:

"I'm worried about the lack of security at the bank, Adam."

"Yeah," he agreed. "I don't like that anyone can walk right in there and open the safe now that the lock's broke."

Susannah held the back of her hand to her forehead. "Land's sake! How much money do you reckon is in the safe?"

Adam whistled and rubbed his chin. "I'd guess a hundred thousand, easy. Maybe even more considering all the money Roderick Mason must have deposited."

"I hear Mr. Taylor hired the blacksmith to fix the safe next Monday, so that's a relief at least."

Despite Susannah's and Adam's appalling lack of acting skills, Johnny's greed was such that he believed the story they fed him. The marshal and his deputy took care of the rest. They staked out the bank around the clock and caught Johnny in the act of trying to rob it the Sunday before the lock was supposedly due to be fixed.

Roderick and Betsy moved to Sacramento, feeling about a hundred sixty pounds lighter and excited to start their new life together. The bustling California city was the perfect location for them in both size and location. Roderick worked for Florence's uncle for a year before branching out and establishing his own firm. Included in his many accomplishments was designing the Neo-classical structure of the California State Capitol at the west end of Capitol Park.

Betsy and Roderick brought into the world four children. Their oldest decided at age eighteen that she didn't want to be courted by any of the gentlemen in her circle of acquaintances. They were boring, she tearfully explained to her father, and she could guess exactly how the rest of her life would go if she married one of them. Her words resonated somewhere in the back of Roderick's memory. With his blessing, she married a cowboy from out of town. That cowboy's name was Caleb Harrington.

The Harringtons and Masons didn't need their children's marriage as an excuse to stay in touch. The Masons returned to Virginia City often to visit the Harringtons and Betsy's parents, a journey made more convenient when they purchased an automobile in 1915.

No one can be right all the time, and Roderick ended up being very wrong about one thing. He'd predicted that Betsy would continue to run and he'd continue to have to chase her, but that wasn't the case. The day they married was the day Roderick was successful in catching Betsy—forever.

The End

Dear Reader,

Thank you for purchasing *Catching Betsy*. If you enjoyed this book, I invite you to sign up for my newsletter to get future book-release alerts, giveaways, and exclusive excerpts. My newsletter subscribers are the first to know about my book sales and freebies too. Sign up now by visiting my website, ameliasmarts.com.

Amelia Smarts

Books by Amelia Smarts

Mail-Order Grooms Series
Handling Susannah
Catching Betsy
Justice for Elsie

Lost and Found in Thorndale Series
Bringing Trouble Home
When He Returns

Tender Alpha Cowboy Romance
Corralling Callie
Fetching Charlotte Rose
The Unbraiding of Anna Brown

Dominant Daddies
Daddy Takes Charge
Cowboy Daddies: Two Western Romances
His Little Red Lily

Steamy, High-Heat Western Romance
Emma's Surrender
Claimed by the Mountain Man

About Amelia Smarts

Amelia Smarts is a *USA Today* bestselling author who writes kinky romance novels containing domestic discipline, spanking, and Dominance/submission. Usually her stories involve a cowboy, and they always involve a man's firm hand connecting with a woman's naughty backside. Amelia holds graduate and undergraduate degrees in creative writing and English. She loves to read, which allows her writing to be influenced by many different genres in addition to romance, including mystery, adventure, history, and suspense.

Amelia's accolades include:

- Golden Flogger Award Finalist for Best BDSM Book (Emma's Surrender)
- Voted #1 Favorite Historical Romance Author in The Bashful Bookwhore's Poll
- Winner: Best Sweet Spanking Romance (Fetching Charlotte Rose) in the Spanking Romance Reviews Reader's Poll
- Runner-up: Best Historical Western Romance (Claimed by the Mountain Man) in the Spanking Romance Reviews Reader's Poll

To learn more about Amelia and her books, visit ameliasmarts.com.

Made in United States
Orlando, FL
17 June 2024

47991024R00093